The Carrot and the Mule

Joseph Anthony Foti

PublishAmerica
Baltimore

© 2002 by Joseph Anthony Foti.
All rights reserved. No part of this book may be reproduced in any form without written permission from the publishers, except by a reviewer who may quote brief passages in a review to be printed in a newspaper or magazine.

First printing

ISBN: 1-59129-757-5
PUBLISHED BY PUBLISHAMERICA BOOK
PUBLISHERS
www.publishamerica.com
Baltimore

Printed in the United States of America

To my precious son Kai and my darling wife Tameka, whose unwavering faith in my abilities provided me the strength to pursue my dream.

SAILING

The icy December rain pelted my eyes as I tried to keep my 500 foot yacht from slamming into the jagged Nantucket rocks. Despite my efforts, the howling night winds, raging sea, and dense fog made steering almost impossible. This was by far the worst storm I had encountered in thirteen years of sailing. Standing at the helm, forced to endure Maurice's mocking glances, I watched helplessly as twenty foot waves crashed continually around the yacht. One good hit would surely plunge us into watery graves.

"This is all your fault, Maurice," I screamed, grabbing him by the head and flinging him into the sea.

"What have I become?" I yelled. I could not believe what I had just done. Maurice was my trusted confidant. He was an eight-inch-tall toy cow, a present from my deceased grandmother and the only childhood toy I had ever received. When I pressed his stomach, he would moo three times.

Standing there soaked and battered, it dawned upon me that I had become what I despised, a scapegoater.

"No more!" I yelled, howling at the heavens. "I will not lose my *Inner Peace*."

The waves kept tossing the yacht in the air and throwing it back at the dark blue sea, completely disregarding its value.

My yacht was the fruit of years of suffering. The abusive childhood, the years of manual labor in a dank warehouse. I will never forget those seemingly endless hours spent dragging heavy boxes and stocking filthy bins with ballet shoes, my lungs filling with soot from the sealed vents, while my hands mingled in blood and dirt at the age of ten. Yet, none of that mattered now as the sea prepared to cancel all bets.

My yacht was my sanctuary. It was the only place on Earth where I felt truly safe. It had cost me nearly five million dollars to build and every detail was to my specifications. The bow was that of a nineteenth century cutter ship. It was sleek and sharp, enabling it to glide through the waves with almost mocking simplicity. The cabin was designed to resemble the banquet room of a seventeenth century French chateau, sabers and all. The bathroom had a marble tub with gold fixtures and was showered in fresh cut lilies and red roses. Even the dinghy had golden oars and diamond engravings. However, none of this mattered now as God prepared to once again destroy my only source of joy.

The waves pounded the deck, tore apart the waterproof doors, and rushed into the hull. Leaving the wheel, I started up the pumps and ran down into the cabin, searching for something to block the doorway with.

It was a situation of my own making. I should have hired a crew, but I had let my distrust of humanity get the better of me. At worst I thought they would kill me in my sleep and sell the yacht, at best I figured they would defecate in my breakfast. No, I had bought *Inner Peace* to escape them, bringing them along would have defeated the purpose. Nonetheless, right now I could have used them. "No, matter," I told myself. "Self-reliance has always been my forte."

I was determined not to lose the yacht. After losing my darling Sara, I vowed to never again care about something to the extent that God's taking it from me would have any effect on me. Nevertheless, having taken Sara, God was after my final pleasure, my yacht which I named *Inner Peace*. The sky thundered ominously, each hot flash a reminder of God's absolute control.

The cold black sea poured into the cabin, quickly shorting out the engines and flooding the pumps. With the power totally gone, I realized the yacht was doomed. As the water started to fill the cabin, I blindly waded around searching for the armoire. Nearly cracking my head on it, I rummaged through the top draw, grabbing some old photos and letters from Sara. I had told myself I was over Sara, naively believing that the greatest betrayal of my life could be forgotten.

Unfortunately, with each pounding wave it all came roaring back to me. My yacht, my plane, my beautiful estates; White Acre, Black Acre, Green Acre, and Blue Acre. They had all been designed to make me forget.

Emerging from the cabin, I put the photos and letters in a pouch on my life vest, climbed into the dinghy and started up the motor. As it pulled away, I watched the ocean pummel *Inner Peace*, tossing it up into the air one final time before slamming it down in an explosion of wind and water. Enraged, the waves knocked me to the side of the dinghy, like a spoiled child playing in the tub. When I looked up *Inner Peace* was no more. The motor of the dinghy quickly flooded and died leaving me to God's fury.

The lightning lit the sky an eerie crimson as I reached into my life jacket and pulled out a photo of my long lost Sara. Gazing upon it, I realized that the sea could no longer shield me from my misery. Throughout my life, the sea had always been my protector. I could swim freely or go to the bow of *Inner Peace* and look up into the purple and orange sky as the wind washed through my hair, seemingly cleansing my soul.

Now the sea was no longer peaceful and every wave battered me with her memory. Suddenly it dawned on me how both the sea and Sara were alike. They were both part of God's ultimate game and I had been too stupid to realize it. There was a time when Sara had made me feel as happy and carefree as the ocean breeze in my hair. Just being in her presence or hearing her voice filled me with pure euphoria. That is true love. That is an experience most people will never have and could never understand. Sadly, just like the sea, that sweet gentle breathtaking woman had turned on me with just as much fury and far less of a warning.

THE MEETING

Nearly a quarter century has passed since our first meeting, yet I still remember it as if it were yesterday. One look into those hazel eyes electrified me with that same jolt of ecstasy I felt when that first blast of cold sea air had hit my hair so many years before. No one else would ever lift my heart to such heights.

I was born Roger Williams, the first son and second child to a sanitation worker in Queens, New York. My father was a devout Catholic and child abuser. He would beat me before church, sit down for the hour mass and then beat me afterwards. My mother, although physically there, had long been gone. In her mind she had a happy loving family and nothing bad ever happened. While being the first son in many families brings love and admiration, in mine it brought hatred. I was a symbol of opportunity lost. A daily reminder of every dream this bitter man had been too gutless to follow. I was his scapegoat, hence beating me was like beating the world. My childhood was thus a long and miserable one, although it was at this time that I first fell in love with the sea.

With my mother in another world, my only protector was my grandmother. During one of her visits the truth came out, as she watched in shock as my father burst through the door with his belt drawn and started viciously beating my face with the heavy metal belt buckle. His face went from bright red to dark purple, the hate raging in his eyes as he furiously tried to cut my eyes out with his buckle.

"Get off him, you psycho," my grandmother screamed, knocking him off me with her cane. "He's five years old. He didn't do anything. He was just coloring in his book."

"You bitch," he howled, charging at her like a mad bull, only to be knocked to the floor by a well-placed shot to the knees from her cane.

"Mom!" my mother yelled, walking in on the madness. "What did you do?" she shouted as she ran to tend to my attacker.

"He was trying to kill Roger," she protested.

"Oh, you're exaggerating," my mother scoffed as she helped him to his chair.

"He's your son, what the hell were you thinking?" my grandmother screamed, adrenaline still rushing through her.

"Don't buy his innocent act. He's no angel," my father bellowed. "He thinks he's better than me. Anyway, he's my son, I'll beat him whenever I feel like it. That's all he's good for anyway!" he barked.

"There, there," my mother soothingly stated. "Eat your dinner before it gets cold," she chirped, placing a gigantic bowl of spaghetti and meatballs in front of his face. "See, Mom," she countered cheerfully as he immediately began scarfing it down like some crazed animal. "No need to make something out of nothing. Just fill his plate and he'll calm right down."

Horrified, my grandmother was faced with a difficult decision. Either report him, thereby subjecting her daughter to legal ramifications or spend the rest of her life raising a child. She chose the latter. Hence, whenever I didn't have school, I stayed with her.

My grandparents had come to this country fleeing poverty and political oppression, just to be greeted with bigotry and hatred. Wisely my grandmother paid little credence to both those bigots who claimed to hate her as well as those who claimed to love her simply because of her roots. My grandfather on the other hand failed to follow her lead. He was determined to prove his naysayers wrong, while rewarding those who supposedly had faith in him. Sadly in his attempt to expose them as frauds, he let them choose his destiny. He spent every waking hour of his life working in his hardware store, not wanting to be viewed as a failure. In order to save the five dollar delivery charge, he would carry sinks and cabinets on his back through the streets to his customers, all by himself. Sadly, treating his body like a mule in order to save that five dollars cost him his life.

One night while carrying an entire living room set on his back, he suffered a massive heart attack and collapsed on the curb. This tragedy brought the bigots together as they literally tore the clothes from his back, robbing him of his last dime and leaving him to die alone like a dog in the night.

My grandmother learned from his death and never trusted anyone again. She repeatedly warned me to be wary of those that profess their love too quickly. She taught me never to let the clamoring of the masses determine what I would become. On a happier note it was she who introduced me to the sea.

At the age of five while most children played with their toys, I drew the sea. My grandmother would take me down to the seaport and sit there knitting, as I spent hours drawing everything I saw. The sea enchanted me with both its vast beauty and deep complexity. Its ultimate lesson being that greatness lies below the surface. Those who understood this and respected it were shown great beauty and power, while those who mocked it suffered the same fate as the *H.M.S. Titanic*.

My first experience with its splendor came courtesy of a twenty-five cent ride on the Staten Island ferry. I remember running to the bow and being greeted by that first gust of crisp sea air in my hair. It was there at the age of five that I first experienced the feeling of pure happiness and not until I met Sara, eighteen years later, would a person ever equal that purity.

Unfortunately, my grandmother, a woman who never smoked or drank, would succumb to cancer, thus leaving me to face the world alone at the age of nine. The victim of an unscrupulous doctor, whose fervor for pharmaceutical kickbacks superseded his duty to warn his patients that the hormone replacement therapy he prescribed for menopausal hot flashes was a known carcinogen.

Immediately following the funeral, my mother found me a job as a box boy, thus initiating me into the wonderful world of manual labor. Although I hated treating my body like a mule, the job did have its benefits. It kept me away from my father and ultimately provided me with the means to flee that world. At age eighteen my hard work paid off, as I escaped to a small New England University where I earned my degree. From there I went on to law school, where I met Sara.

After finishing college, I was accepted into one of the best law schools in New England and I should have been thrilled; however, I was not. Those around me, supposed friends and well wishers, talked about it as some great achievement and of course tried to take credit for it. To me, however, it meant nothing. My childhood had taught me three lessons. Never trust anyone, every choice has a cost, and never celebrate before a task is done. The ultimate goal was graduating, passing the bar and becoming rich and powerful. None of these steps had been completed yet so there was nothing to celebrate.

This is one of humanity's problems. People always spend the profits before they have them and then cry like children and expect help and pity when things fall apart. I never expected anything from anyone and thus blamed only myself for my failures or successes.

I had met Sara at the beginning of my first year of law school, nearly a quarter century ago, at an orientation dinner. Most people use these occasions to assess who they deem usable or "network," as it's called. I was there for the free food only although nothing is really free. The price I expected to pay for this meal was a night spent with lying vultures, casting their false smiles while secretly plotting to use me for anything they could get out of me. To my surprise at this gathering of vultures I would find an angel.

She stood in the center of the room and was surrounded by every male there, from the delivery boys to the drooling retired professors. All with one goal and one goal only. I went over of course to see what could compel these highly touted legal minds to act like drooling mongrels. Sadly, I had always been disappointed because although I usually found some toothpick like goddess in a tight dress, one look in her eyes always ruined it for me. While they saw a trophy to obtain, I found a shallow pathetic creature who's supposed beauty did nothing for me. I unfortunately could see the woman beneath the facade and it always disgusted me.

I'm not saying that in the past I had not chased creatures like this. After all this is what society tells you to want. In the past I had tolerated shallow girls like this mostly to be the envy of my supposed friends, yet the intended goal brought little joy. Many a time I would lie awake in bed while one of these supposed goddesses slept at my side. Ironically instead of an afterglow I would feel nauseous. My sole want would be for morning to come and take with it this wretched creature. None of these empty conquests could ever compare to the pleasure I felt that morning when I was five years old and the ocean wind blew through my hair as I stood at the bow of the ferry.

All this changed, that late September night, almost twenty-five years ago. As I made my way through the masses, my eyes fell upon what I expected to be just another shell of a woman. Alas to my amazement, I found something I had never come across before or since then.

Physically she was petite and stunning just like all the rest. However, when I looked into those hazel eyes, I felt the rush of the sea in my hair. She smiled at me just like everyone else, although the greeting I gave her was something she did not expect. While every degenerate there insulted her intelligence with transparent come ons, I refused to sully my soul for the chance at a mere dalliance. I simply asked her name, introduced myself as Roger and quickly withdrew to the window to get some air. The experience had knocked the breath out of me and I wanted to clear my head; however, she would not allow it. Spotting me at the window, she brushed away the rabid dogs chasing her and came over. We went outside to escape the ever growing mob, stood in the pouring rain, and talked the entire night away; shielded from the horny toads that dared not risk their precious clothes.

"So, taking a break?" She laughed.

"Won't your minions miss you?" I replied.

"Oh, please," she said with a sigh. "I thought law school would be different, but it's not. They're supposed to be wiser but they're just as selfish as everyone else. I came here tonight hoping to enjoy stimulating conversation with some great legal minds, only to find a bunch of horny old men, spouting pathetic come ons. What's worse is that the few female lawyers here are avoiding me like the plague because of them."

"Well, that's what you get for having expectations," I answered slyly.

"It's refreshing to finally meet someone who'd rather risk ruining a perfectly good suit than miss out on a rainstorm. What are you a 'the'?"

"A what?" I said quite confused.

"A 'the,' she replied. "You know, like Charles the second or Henry the third. Someone who's here on daddy's dollar. Are you Roger 'the' anything?" she said with a smile.

"No, I'm not a 'the,'" I replied a bit annoyed. "I'm here because I earned it. My father wouldn't pay for high school, never mind law school. Not that it's any of your business," I stated frankly. "What about you? Are you daddy's little princess?" I countered coyly.

"Hardly," she said with a smile. "I had to work for it, just like you. So, then; who are you?"

"I'm just a guy who likes the rain," I replied.

"Well, I guess that makes us kindred spirits," she chirped.

At the end of the evening, I walked her home and said goodnight. I was so taken I didn't even ask for her number. This was a first for her. No guy had ever spent time with her and not hit on her. This seeming indifference unwittingly made me appear strange and exciting to her, hence setting in motion the most painful betrayal of my life.

I didn't see Sara again for over a month and tried to convince myself that she wasn't different. That she was just like everyone else. I might have been successful had she not forced the issue. Usually if I wanted someone out of my life I just ignored them for a couple of weeks and they were gone. This was not the case with Sara. About a month after our meeting I received a call from her late one November night.

When I asked how she got my number, she just smirked and said, "I have my ways."

Over the next couple of months we talked often, as each conversation made the attempt to classify her as just another user and write her off, more and more impossible.

After one of her calls, I turned to Maurice who was sitting on my desk and asked, "What do you think of her?"

I picked him up and pressed his belly, hearing three moos.

"No, don't worry, Maurice," I assured him, "she's not like the others. Sara is like no other woman I have ever met," I told him.

"Most women fall under two categories. Either they are very emotional and kind or heartless and strong. The emotional while kind and good-natured are often swallowed whole by the vultures in our society. This is due to the fact that they lack the strength and vindictiveness it takes to defend themselves. On the other hand the strong often lose their heart and everything becomes, 'What can you do for me now.'

"While the strong are definitely survivors, there is nothing inside them. When I look into their eyes, I see a cold and bitter person who sickens me, thus I want nothing to do with them. Sara is neither of these women," I stated happily.

"Moo, moo, moo," I heard.

"You don't believe me, do you, Maurice?" I said with a smile. "I understand your doubt. I was skeptical at first too, but now I know better.

"Sara possesses a warm and loving nature, hence she's capable of caring deeply about others without having an ulterior motive. It's perhaps her greatest quality and the reason I love her. Nevertheless, Sara is also very strong and can eat the users up and spit them out when she wants to. Many people consider her to be cold and aloof; however, they are usually the same sardonic twits whose facades she had seen through," I argued to my cow.

"Her ability to see through the lies of the masses just adds to the pile of traits we share. Even when she is in her strong defensive lawyer mode, her kind and loving nature is still in her eyes and it's her eyes that hold me at her will," I explained. "No one has ever been able to control me like she can. All it takes is one look into those eyes and I am at her mercy, Maurice." I then sat Maurice back on the desk.

If you're wondering, no, I'm not insane. I didn't believe that Maurice was actually alive. Talking to him was just my way of dispelling any doubts. It was a form of therapy. Instead of hitting a punching bag, I talked to a toy cow. This latest exercise had succeeded in its goal. I now trusted Sara.

By the end of our first school year, we were almost inseparable. We would go out to dinner, afterwards taking in a movie or a show. That summer we both found jobs in our intended profession. She as an intern in a real estate firm and I as an intern in the district attorney's office. Ironically I was placed in their child abuse department.

One late August night, near the end of our first summer together, I finally had the honor of meeting the Ravenports. Sara had been their live-in nanny since college and continued to do so during law school in order to get free room and board. They were from the baby boomer generation and had been big drug abusers during the 1960s. Luckily for them, they didn't have to worry about making money. Mr. Ravenport had come from a long line of extremely wealthy men. His great grandfather had come to this country practically penniless, yet by the end of his life with hard work and dedication, he amassed a fortune in the shipbuilding industry. His grandfather parlayed that fortune into the steel and railroad industries and his father became a giant in the meat industry. Thus the Ravenports could have lived seven lifetimes without money becoming an issue.

Sadly, money won't shield you from your own stupidity. Their drug abuse had basically fried their brains, causing them to forget how to do the most simple tasks. They would go for weeks without bathing and often forgot to lock the door or where they had put the car. This obviously made raising a child difficult and thus where Sara had come in.

Sara despised the Ravenports. Although they had put a roof over her head and food in her mouth, it was simply payment for raising their child. What upset her the most was their constant onslaught of mind games. They would pretend to care about her and often treated her like a member of the family one moment, just to treat her like a servant the next. Although she would never admit this to anyone including me, this constant yanking of her proverbial emotional chain devastated her. She would complain about it but then deny why it really bothered her.

That August night, as I was about to meet the couple who had given her so much financially and taken so much emotionally, I felt both pity and rage. One part of me said put on your happy face and greet them nicely, while the other wanted to rip off their heads and use them as bowling balls with the oncoming traffic. As I walked up the steps of their million dollar brownstone, I tried to ready myself for the users I was about to meet. Growing up in an abusive environment, I had met many strange characters, yet nothing could prepare me for what I was about to encounter.

THE RAVENPORTS

Sara used her key to open the cast iron door and in we went. There in the living room sitting in two wicker chairs were the Ravenports. The house was a work of art in itself. It was a nineteenth century brownstone with high ceilings, tall windows, and wooden floors. The room was surrounded by an oak bookcase which housed many of the supposedly "in" books of their time. However, living in an expensive house and surrounding yourself with great literature and art will not turn a toad into a butterfly. A simple truth they would never be able to shake.

As they sat in their chairs, I glanced over these dismal creatures. Mr. Ravenport was about fifty years old. He was bald and grossly overweight. His chin dripped down off his face resembling the point of a rhinoceros. His eyes were covered by a pair of old thick glasses, worn perhaps to conceal the pathetic creature which loomed within.

"So, what have you been doing to our Sara?" He laughed.

"Just plotting your death," I replied.

The old man gulped swallowing his chin not knowing whether to laugh or run.

Sara just looked at them smirking for a bit until she was convinced that they were indeed worried, at which time she quickly shouted out, "Oh, he's just kidding. Stop being funny, Roger."

"Oh, yes, very amusing," Mr. Ravenport replied trying to fake a laugh.

"Yes, very comical," Mrs. Ravenport quickly chimed in. "So our Sara tells us you're going to be a lawyer. Better practice lying now," she said with a laugh.

"Why? Have you had any bad experiences with lawyers?" I asked.

"No, it's just that their breed are perpetual liars, everybody knows that," she answered smugly.

"Have you ever known a lawyer?" I responded angrily.

"No," she replied, "But…"

"But nothing," I interrupted. "You shouldn't talk about something you know nothing about."

"You don't have to be rude," she answered back looking quite hurt.

"Oh, Roger, stop being funny; he's just playing with you," Sara quickly remarked.

"Oh," Mrs. Ravenport replied. "Would you like something to drink?"

"No, I have to be going," I stated happily.

"Oh, you probably have a lot of studying to do," she said with a rushed smile.

"Yes, something like that," I replied.

As she got up to shake my hand goodbye, I realized that I had been so preoccupied observing Mr. Ravenport and Sara's reaction to him, that I had failed to take a conscious look at Mrs. Ravenport. When she rose from her chair, I reexamined the scene and was shocked at what I saw. She looked to be in her late forties. Her hair was short and worn, probably from over bleaching. Her face was full of wrinkles and her eyes were wide and glassy, indicating someone who was not quite "all there." When I looked down, I saw why. She was wearing an old stained maternity dress with a large parcel bulging beneath it. I had not noticed it while she was sitting down, but now up it was there for all to see. It looked to be an old bag of flour. I could make out an F and an L through parts of her worn out dress.

"Oh, Sara didn't tell you the good news? We're expecting," she said looking quite serious.

"Oh," I managed to mumble. "Well, I have to go now." I shook both of their hands and turned to Sara, who had been smirking quite devilishly the entire time and said, "Will you please walk me out?"

"Sure," she chirped happily. Once outside I turned to her and shouted, "What was that?"

"Whatsoever do you mean?" she replied with a sparkle in her eyes.

"You know exactly what I mean and wipe that smirk off your face. What is that bundle she is carrying?"

"Oh that," she replied quite mischievously. "Didn't I tell you about her sack?"

"No, you didn't," I answered vehemently.

"Well, Barbara and Tim did a lot of drugs in the sixties and seventies which made them both sterile. When Barbara found out she lost it and went into a deep denial, buying maternity dresses and strapping a sack of flour to her stomach. She insists that she's pregnant and won't even drink or smoke anymore. That's why they adopted Susie. Tim went all the way down to Peru and paid off some poor village woman to give them her daughter."

"Why Peru?" I asked.

"I don't know," she replied. "Maybe he was afraid that the mother might change her mind and try to get the kid back. Perhaps putting a continent between them makes him feel safer," she responded matter-of-factly.

"Why didn't you tell me any of this?" I asked.

"You never asked me," she giggled.

"Stop being smart," I barked, gently kissing her goodnight as the rains began to soak us.

"Call me when you get home," she gently pleaded.

"I will," I replied as once again I became lost in her eyes. As I walked home utterly drenched by the heavens, I could not get over how such a kind loving person could exist in a world filled with insincere apathy.

As soon as I arrived home, I called her and we picked up right where we left off.

"You should have told me about her sack," I said.

"Well, it's an odd thing to talk about," she replied. "Anyway, their sterility is their own fault. Mrs. Ravenport told me that the only reason she took drugs in the first place was because, 'it was the in thing to do at the time.'"

That sentence in a nutshell explains the Ravenports. Everything they did in their life was done to please others. Unfortunately, most people are like this. They never consider the consequences of their actions until it's too late. Even then, all they care about is finding a scapegoat to take the blame. People like this sicken me. Their eyes are filled with nothing but selfishness and emptiness. Their only contributions to this world are neglected children. If they can't have them, they buy them; not to share their love and kindness I remind you, but because it is the "in thing to do." This blind adherence to vogue is why the Ravenports adopted Susie and why Mrs. Ravenport carried her sack.

Unfortunately what these idiots failed to realize is that nothing in life is free, everything comes with a price. The price for their ignorance was their barrenness. Pathetically, unlike the dimmest child, they refused to learn from their mistakes or take responsibility for their actions. Nevertheless, pretending the boulder's not bearing down upon you will not save you from getting squashed. The clearest example of this is Mrs. Ravenport's sack of flour.

The end of summer brought with it our second year in law school and for Sara, the envy of the Ravenports. The beginning of classes meant an onslaught of research and writing, which left Sara little time to humor the Ravenports. They had put up with her work in the past because I guess having a law student as their live-in baby sitter had made them the envy of all their friends. As time passed, however, this uniqueness began to ware thin, bringing their true nature bubbling to the surface.

Sara spent many hours in her room with the door closed studying. They didn't mind that she was not amusing Susie. What upset the Ravenports most was that she was not amusing them. They looked upon her as sort of their own personal court jester, existing only to amuse them. This really hurt Sara because she cared very much for Susie and for some strange reason seemed to care about the Ravenports. She had tried to make herself believe it when they told her that, "They considered her to be part of the family." With each passing day, however, their red-herring became harder to swallow.

They would come home from work and demand that she go to their friends' parties. As if sitting in a room with a bunch of self-centered wannabe status seekers, as old men relentlessly hit on her, was something she would actually enjoy.

She had put up with it in the past as the price for free rent and board; however, she was not going to let them destroy her career. She soon began to realize that this might actually be their true motive. Soon after her refusal to go to the party, life with the Ravenports started to become unbearable. One night near the end of the semester, I called her just to be greeted by a shrill sound emanating from the other side.

"Sara, what's with all the noise?" I asked.

"It's them," she whimpered. "They know finals are coming up soon, so this is retribution for not going to their parties. I feel like a goldfish swimming in a bowl of acid."

"Don't let them get to you, that's what they want," I told her. "Sara, you have to be strong," I pleaded.

To avoid the immediate situation, she began studying at my apartment. This only made the situation worse. They began filling her plate with foods they knew could kill her. As an added bonus they began insisting that she sit with them at their dinner table even if she had already eaten and every chance they had, mocked her choice of career and the fact that she was not already a "big time lawyer."

These actions adversely began effecting me as well, since most of my time was spent consoling Sara and trying to make her feel special. Something which became harder and harder with each ensuing day. I began to fall behind in my studies, but it did not matter to me as Sara had become my entire world. Nothing else mattered but her. Two weeks before finals she arrived home just to be greeted by a barrage of complaints.

"You never do anything with us," Mrs. Ravenport whined.

"That's because I have finals approaching," Sara replied respectfully.

"I don't want to hear it," Mrs. Ravenport screeched. "Either start pulling your weight or get out."

That night Sara came to my door in tears. It would be the first of many such trips. "What's wrong?" I asked.

Relaying the whole sordid ordeal, she began sobbing uncontrollably. "Roger, it's all hogwash. Truth be told, I spend much more time with Susie than they do. I'm the one who took her to the museum and I'm the one who's always pestering her to read books."

"Did you tell them that?" I asked.

"Of course," she replied.

"What was their response?" I retorted.

"They denied it," she shouted exasperated. "They actually accused me of trying to turn Susie against them and Barbara said that I was the reason that she hasn't given birth yet."

"You can't let them get to you. You have to be patient," I pleaded as I held her tightly.

"I know," she yawned. "It's just exhausting." She smiled as I gently cradled her to sleep in my arms.

The beginning of December brought with it the Ravenports' latest blitz on her career. Right before finals they insisted that Sara start paying rent for the little room she had, knowing full well that she could not afford it. This was done purely to upset her in the hopes that she would fail out of law school and be forced to become their nanny forever.

That night I sat in the park and watched as a pack of rats tore apart a nightingale, just as it began to sing its divine song. I refused to let a similar fate befall Sara. I paid her rent thus focusing her attention off the Ravenports and on to her studies. This of course infuriated the Ravenports and made them despise me even more, but I could not care less. Sara was the only person that mattered to me.

My efforts paid off, as she did well on her exams to the dismay of the Ravenports. Sara spent that Christmas with her family in Paris, thus leaving me to suffer without the one I loved. This did not really upset me though, because I was strong-willed and cared only about what was best for her. I actually encouraged her to go, even though it meant abandoning me to another holiday spent with my abusive

family.
    That holiday season turned out better than I expected, as we spent almost every moment of it on the phone with one another.

APRIL

As soon as she returned from her visit, we began searching for an apartment of her own. She needed someplace safe from the clutches of the conniving Ravenports. In under a month I had found her a place and she was thrilled. Having a place of her own to call home made her feel very independent. She decorated it and it appeared to make her happy. This in turn made me happy.

This happiness was not to be long lived, however. It was sort of God's way of hanging a carrot in front of my mouth just to yank it away if I tried to bite it. My biggest mistake was trusting her too much. In the past no one had ever warranted that sort of trust. This is understandable considering that my first candidates were an abusive father and a mother living in a fantasy world. Sara, however, was different. She had a pure heart, a kind soul, and tremendous inner strength and cunning. These were the attributes which made me notice her in the first place and the main reason why I loved and trusted her. A mistake I ultimately would live to regret. I should have known that such a beautiful woman would eventually be swayed by the users of our society. Unfortunately I believed her when she said she loved me and shut my eyes to anything to the contrary. My faith in her was total and I refused to believe that anyone could sway her against me.

The first sway showed up at Sara's door one early June night, soon after the end of our second year of law school. We had just come from dinner and a show and were going back to her place when I first met April.

She sat on the front step of the building. She was about five foot five and had bleached blond hair. I guess many men would have found her attractive in a whorish sort of way. She wore a tiny tank top, that left nothing to the imagination and the smallest mini skirt I had ever seen.

My first thought was that this was a prostitute waiting for her john, but Sara's cries of, "April, what are you doing here?" soon cleared up that notion.

They embraced at which point she said, "Hi, Sara, I felt like Paris was getting old and missed you so much since Christmas that I had to come over."

"Oh, April, this is Roger," Sara stated.

"Well, well, well, I finally get to meet Roger. So how are you, superman?" she asked with a smirk.

"Who are you?" I sarcastically retorted.

"Roger, this is my friend, April, from Paris. We practically grew up together," Sara explained.

"Oh, hi," I replied.

"Not much of a talker, is he?" she snickered.

"Make yourself useful and carry my bags up to Sara's apartment," she ordered.

"She's staying with you?" I asked, totally ignoring April's command.

"Oh, didn't I tell you? Last Christmas I invited her to come stay with me whenever she was in the country."

"No, you didn't," I shot back.

"I must have forgotten," Sara replied.

Right then I should have known something was awry because Sara never forgot anything. Still I trusted her and didn't want to upset her. I carried April's bags upstairs, resulting in Sara's kissing me goodnight and saying that April probably was tired and should get to bed. Always the loving soul, I honored her wishes and left them to sleep.

In the three weeks that April stayed with her, Sara and I only spoke once. Her excuse was that she was just playing the good host, but I should have spotted how quickly she would put another person's needs over mine. Unfortunately, my heart refused to hear what my mind was shouting. That she would put her desire to be with me on hold in order to care for a friend in need was just another example of her kind nature. Sadly, I had failed to consider the notion that perhaps this was not such a sacrifice, an error I would later pay for.

Having been without Sara for three weeks, my spirits began to somber. In an attempt to free myself from this ill mood, I went down to the campus lake and sat on a rock overlooking the water. For some strange reason sitting by water always seemed to cheer me up. This newfound tranquility was quickly dissolved by the sounds of someone approaching. It was Sara.

"There you are, Roger," she shouted. "I thought I'd find you here," she said with a smile.

"Dr. Livingstone, I presume," I slyly retorted.

"Very funny, Roger. It hasn't been that long."

"So, Where's your partner in crime?" I joked.

"Please don't mention that twit. I just dropped her off at the airport. Roger, you have no idea what I had to endure these past three weeks. All she wanted to do is go clubbing and pick up guys. She doesn't seem to appreciate the difficulty in becoming a lawyer. She wanted to go out every night and kept pestering me, even after I told her that I had too much work to do. She made my life a living hell, Roger," she pleaded, throwing her arms around me and hopping onto my lap.

"Where did you meet such a shrew?" I bluntly queried.

"I met her in grade school," she replied.

"Why are you still friends with her? She seems a bit self-centered," I said with a smile.

"Well, we share a common bond. We both were abandoned by our fathers at an early age," she stated matter-of-factly.

"I'm sorry," I said.

"Don't be. It's not your fault," she replied. "Anyway I'm fine with it. April's the one who can't handle it. I was lucky, my father left when I was an infant so I never really missed him. April's leech of a father abandoned her when she was five years old. What makes it so sad is that while my mother was very loving, April's mom took it out on her."

"Why?" I asked.

"Because she's a scapegoater, Roger. You know the type. Anyway, when her father bailed on them, her mother had to quit college and take up a job as a janitor in order to support them. Refusing to take the blame for her own shallow choices, her mother like a true scapegoater focused her anger on April," Sara stated, shaking her head in pity. "What's worse is the effect it had on April."

"Why, what happened?" I asked.

"She let it consume her. While you and I refused to let our miserable childhoods affect us, April just repeated the cycle. She equated her mother's bitterness to the lack of a man, failing to realize that true happiness can only come from within. This is why you and I are so happy, Roger," Sara said with a smile. "We look to one another for someone to share our life, not someone to provide it. April never understood this, no matter how hard I tried to explain it to her. She just kept lying on her back searching for that knight in shining armor who would provide instant happiness. It's sad because this pipe dream of hers has made her a very superficial and weak person, as well as quite the slut," she stated frankly.

"Oh, really," I replied trying to act surprised.

"Yes, really," she countered sternly. "It's not funny, Roger. She's twenty-seven and still living at home. She has no job and was just dumped by some loser she's been spreading them for."

It appeared that April had quite a history of putting out and then getting dumped. Sara blamed her for it.

"In the past there have been guys who really cared about her, but April is so superficial that she just laughed at them. Instead she wastes her time chasing no talent actors and singers. This was the twenty-seventh guy in the last two years to have his way with her and then dump her. She's pathetic, she never learns," Sara scoffed.

"Where does she find all these winners?" I asked with a smirk.

"Oh please, Roger, you know as well as I do that the world is full of vermin, all looking to sink their teeth into the first girl that comes their way. For example, her last weed was a two bit actor named Jamal, who found her staking out the set of a movie he played an extra in," Sara explained.

"April told me that he took her for a drink at which point she popped out a condom and asked to go back to his hotel room. Jamal enjoyed his little slut until he had his fill, subsequently returning to his wife and kids. After crying for days over the fact that he didn't call her, April found out where he lived and flew there. Once there, she rented a nearby hotel room and then spent the rest of her savings on a rare bottle of wine which she had delivered to his house. On the label she made sure to write her hotel room number. Three days went by and she heard nothing. When she finally got up the nerve to call her Romeo, a woman answered saying that she was his wife and, 'The wine was divine.'

"Jamal showed up at her hotel room that night, but instead of telling him where to go she slept with him. When she called him the next day, he told her that if she didn't stop bothering him he was going to get a restraining order against her. I had to send her the money for a plane ticket home," Sara said with a sigh.

"Since Jamal, there have been many other weeds just like him. Instead of learning from her mistakes and looking for a meaningful relationship, April just keeps treating her body like a drive-through window. I actually pity her," Sara stated sadly. "I've really outgrown her," she added.

"Then why are you still friends with her?" I queried.

"Well, I feel sorry for her," she replied. "The only reason I spend time with her is to comfort her."

"What does she want from you?" I asked warily.

"Roger, stop being so suspicious. She just wants me to validate her behavior by telling her that these parasites really love her."

"Well, do you?" I asked.

"No, Roger, you know I would never say that. I just tell her that she has to move on with her life and forget about all these weeds," she replied adamantly.

What I failed to realize was that April was left with two choices. Either change her lifestyle or get Sara to be just as superficial and sluttish as she was. This way Sara would have to either agree with her or become a hypocrite.

I never in a million years thought this to be a possibility. Just the thought that Sara would ever do something like this to me was unfathomable. First of all, she was too smart to fall for the type of guys April liked. Secondly, she loved me and would never betray me. My love and faith in Sara would ultimately cause the greatest misery of my life. Sadly this was yet to come.

TODD AND MARY

As the Summer neared its end, I had the joy of meeting yet another of my sweet Sara's colorful friends. I remember our first meeting vividly. It was a sweltering August night just three weeks before the start of our third and final year of law school. Had you asked what I thought I'd be doing a year from then, I would have given you the standard answer. Sara and I would be on a world cruise celebrating our passing the bar. After our vacation, I would start my new $100,000 a year job at one of the most prestigious law firms in the country.

That's what I would have told you, but it would have been nothing more than a pure canard. As you should know by now, I've never been a fan of chance. I do not trust it. That's why Sara had been such a surprise. Thus when I thought of my life a year from then I envisioned the worst case scenario. This way I wouldn't be disappointed. Actually I would be quite relieved since I always made my worse case scenario so dependant on things going so impossibly wrong that the prospect of it coming true was as likely as winning the lotto. My worst case scenario at that time was that a year from then I would have failed the bar and still be unemployed, thus unable to give Sara the things she so deserved. My worst case scenario like my life revolved around her. Regrettably, this proved the only time that I'd actually long for my worst case scenario.

As for Todd and Mary, these two people in my mind are yet another thing that is wrong with society. While I always foresaw the worst, Todd always expected the best case scenario to happen. When it didn't work out he always blamed others for it. Mary was the proverbial weak woman. In a generation where women had become strong and heartless, Mary was weak and pathetic. She did everything Todd told her, behaving as if her will and conscience no longer existed.

They lived in a tiny one room apartment, located in an area of the city dubbed, "The killing zone." Todd worked as a cab driver, while Mary popped out one kid after another. They really couldn't afford to take care of themselves, never mind seven children, but that didn't matter to Todd. The night I first met them, we ate at a cheap little diner by the docks. Sara had made the arrangements to fit Todd and Mary's budget.

As we waited for them, Sara could see I was not amused with any of this. I did not like meeting people who would put their own welfare above that of their children. Also the thought of even Sara's shoe touching the floor of this disgusting place really pissed me off. Although sweltering outside, the inside of this little rats' nest made hell seem like a cool breeze. The manager who was shivering in the left corner trying to wipe the vomit off one of the five sweaters he was wearing, had turned the heat on high. From the looks of the burnt spoons on the tables and the track marks around his eyes, this corpse in training obviously missed his favorite poison. Sadly, being a heroin addict leaves little time to follow the health code. While roaches ran commando raids, flies incessantly buzzed in our faces. For everyone we swatted, two more took its place.

Sitting in the right corner sat the grossly overweight health inspector, loudly snorting his bribe. Given this bad omen, I decided to take a peek inside the kitchen. The night just kept getting better, as rats swam in the stew, while a bitter cook enacted his revenge on those that dared be served. Needless to say, Sara and I didn't touch a crumb.

"What kind of man would allow his wife to eat in a place like this?" I asked myself. I would soon find out.

To my surprise in the driveway of this dump arrived a brand new jeep carrying Todd and Mary. Todd wanted us to come out and see his new toy. He was proud of it. He said it had cost him $40,000 and was the new top of the line model. This despite the fact that he already owned a Jeep that was just two years old and Mary drove the car her mother gave her. As we sat down, I was face to face with a man who would spend $40,000 on a new Jeep, yet had no problem bringing his wife to a place like this.

After the initial introductions, Mary had a surprise for us. She was expecting her seventh child just three months after the birth of their first son.

"Do you think it wise to be buying a $40,000 Jeep with your eighth child on the way?" I asked.

"Relax." He grinned. "Everything will work out just fine."

"So, was this a surprise?" Sara asked.

"No way," Todd barked suddenly slamming his hand on the table. "It's all part of the master plan," he replied slyly.

"The master plan?" I asked. "What per se is this master plan you speak of?"

"Well, per se to you too." He laughed. "My master plan is pure genius, Mr. big time lawyer. I'm going to have seven sons, one for every day of the week. That way there will be a great chance of one of them becoming a star athlete and making millions of dollars. Once the boy gets the green, he'll give it all to me," Todd yelled.

"Really," I replied, staring directly at Sara. "So, how goes the collection?" I asked with a smirk.

"Bad," he replied. "I only have six girls and one son. It's not my fault though. This bitch refuses to go along," he explained hitting Mary on the arm. "Then again it's not all her fault." He laughed smacking her ass. "That other bitch has to take some of the blame, but Mary still played a part in it," he griped.

"How?" I queried angrily.

"Well a couple of years back, I decide to spend my paycheck at one of those strip clubs and Mary here started getting on my back. After I beat the bitch, I found some ho on the corner and got me some," Todd explained matter-of-factly. "Nine months later, the ho gave it to stupid here and she actually took it in," he yelled sticking his finger in Mary's face.

Instead of protesting, Mary just apologized to him at which point Todd yelled, "That baby in your belly better be a boy, bitch."

After just sitting there inanely listening to this moron speak, I was ready to take my fork under the table and put an end to his breeding days. Sara, however, saw me and grabbed my hand. I then asked him how he intended to support his little utopia.

He just flexed his arms and yelled, "Don't worry about it. It's all taken care of. I've just been accepted into a community college which gave me a grant to pay for the tuition. Instead of going, I used some of it to get those damn bill collectors off my back and spent the rest on the Jeep," he stated proudly, joking that by the time the school got wise to him, his million dollar sons would pay them off.

I guess the silver lining to his fraud is that because of guys like Todd, schools changed their policies and started applying their grants directly to tuition instead of blindly handing out checks. This is what I meant when I said Todd was the exact opposite of me. While I always prepared for the worst by working hard and saving money, Todd expected to win the lotto every day. Why God would allow such a stupid and selfish man to have such a devoted wife I would never know. Why God had given him so much, while He had given me so little, is something I would never understand. Nevertheless, that night I promised God that everything would be forgiven. I vowed that my entire hideous past would never be mentioned again, if it just gave me Sara. Considering that it had given so many sweet souls to scoundrels like Todd who did not deserve them and actually abused them, my request did not seem too grave. Especially since I pledged to treat her like a queen and always put her needs above my own. In the end God would not even grant me this.

Utterly disgusted, I turned my attention towards Mary. My first impression of her had been that she was pathetic and selfish. Not only did she allow herself to be abused, she also knowingly brought children into an abusive environment. I gazed deeply into her eyes, searching desperately for some glimmer of hope or even an iota of self-respect but found none. All I found was what I had expected to find. Total admiration and love for Todd. There was nothing else there and nothing else mattered. Her mind ceased to exist. Her life was dedicated to doing only what would make Todd happy, no matter the consequences to herself or anyone else. A woman who puts her needs over those of the children she chose to bring into this world deserves to be shot. Yet there I was having dinner with two of the most selfish people I would ever meet.

After our glorious dinner with Todd and Mary, I asked Sara why she would want to spend a minute in the company of a miscreant like Todd.

"He's my friend," she stated bluntly.

"Your friend. What could you possibly have in common with them? How do you even know them?" I shouted dumbfounded.

"I met him in college. I was volunteering at a substance abuse center and Todd was one of the patients they let me work with," she replied nonchalantly.

"Did you become friends with all the addicts?" I asked totally astounded.

"No, Roger, it's just that they were very friendly. Todd called me to thank me for my help and Mary kept calling for advice and gradually we became friends."

"But he's scum," I yelled. "He takes pride in beating his wife, committing fraud, impregnating hookers, and spending his paycheck in a bar. How can you possibly consider him a friend?"

"I know, Roger, but he says he's working on his temper. Anyway I don't like cutting people out of my life."

"Why not? Why burden yourself with those whom on their best day will only offer cheerful indifference?" I shouted.

"I don't know. I guess it has to do with my father abandoning me. Growing up I always felt like I was missing out on things and I don't want to do that to Todd and Mary. But I guess you wouldn't understand, given that your father didn't leave you," she chided cynically.

"No, my father didn't leave!" I shot back. "He stayed around and beat me! At least your father was considerate enough to leave when he realized that he didn't love you. Mine stayed around and drilled home that point every night, while my mother just turned her back pretending it wasn't happening. Of course I understand not wanting to abandon people, but you also have to know when to get out. I didn't just stay there and put up with that crap. I worked hard and found a way out of that world, just like you did. You're too smart to let guys like Todd use you," I pleaded.

"I'm not going to let him use me, Roger. Don't worry about it. If he ever tried something, I'd drop them in a heartbeat," she assured me.

I left her apartment that night with a sinking feeling in my gut. I wondered what Todd expected to get from my Sara. I had my own misgivings just from that meeting. Thoughts I could never share, for she considered him to be her friend. Lamentably, within a year's time my suspicions would prove to be warranted.

THE ABANDONMENT

For Sara, the final year of law school brought with it a fiscal impasse. Her newfound independence had taken its toll on her bank account. Hence, she asked me to loan her some money for rent and food. Of course I obliged. It was a bright sunny day, so after going to the bank we basked in the sunlight and lunched in the park.

"Thanks again, Roger, at least I know one person loves me," she said with a smile.

"You're just realizing that fact," I retorted playfully.

"No. It's just that now I'm sure," she chirped happily.

"How are you doing tuition wise?" I asked.

"Well being a French citizen disqualifies me from any American financial aid, but I did receive a French student loan."

"How much are they giving you?"

"$10,000," she replied. "Leaving me $10,000 short."

"What are you going to do?" I asked a bit worried.

"Don't worry, Roger. You know I always tie up the loose ends. I applied for some private loans and if I can't get them, I'm sure my family and friends will help out."

Unfortunately, when your future relies on your supposed friends, they better be more than just fair weather friends. A truth Sara was about to discover firsthand.

Over that summer, Sara had provided for the fall or so she thought. Immediately after the conclusion of our second year of law school, the Ravenports started bothering her again. They would call her day and night, insisting that she come visit them. Although she should have told these supposed fair weather friends where to go, Sara, not wanting to abandon Susie, visited them every so often.

During one of her visits Mr. Ravenport asked, "How are you going to pay for your final year of school?" knowing full well that she was ineligible for U.S. financial aid.

"I received a French student loan, but I'm still $10,000 short," she replied.

"Why didn't you say so?" he said with a grin. "Barbara and I would be more than happy to give you the remaining $10,000 for the fall semester when it's due," he promised.

That night she came over so happy and carefree.

"See, Roger; I told you everything would work out," she gloated happily.

"Sara, I don't want to put a damper on your parade, yet I have to wonder why they would do this. What do they expect in return?"

"Nothing, Roger. Everything is not always cloak and dagger. There are people in this world who actually do things out of the kindness of their hearts. Tim said that he looked upon me as one of the family and wanted to help," she replied hostilely.

"There may be a rare group of selfless people still alive, but the Ravenports are not part of it. Given their past track record of kicking you when you're down, I wouldn't bank on them," I countered honestly.

"Roger," she yelled. "Your one problem is that you can't trust anyone. Tim and Barbara are just being friendly. Anyway, I didn't ask them for the money, they volunteered to give it to me. If they didn't intend to give it to me, why would they volunteer to do so?"

Regrettably for my sweet Sara, her question would soon be answered.

Three days later their calls became apropos of a stalker. She would return home only to find her answering machine littered with messages from the Ravenports. They were supposedly calling to tell her that Susie missed her and was wondering if she wanted to spend time with her. As Sara was busy with her internships and then April's appearance gave her no time to spend with me, never mind the Ravenports, she politely declined. I proved to be far more understanding. I knew that Sara needed to feel liked, even by those she despised. Although otherwise very intelligent, she wasted far too much time trying to disprove the lies of devils. Hence, she needed to believe that her supposed friends cared about her. Therefore when April came to town, although not particularly thrilled with being tossed on the back burner, I held my tongue. Alas, the maniacal Ravenports proved to be far less compassionate.

They started leaving nasty messages on her answering machine, saying that Susie felt that Sara didn't love her anymore and was very depressed. This Sara knew to be a lie. Although this occurred around the same time that April showed up, Sara always made time to call Susie. Truth be told, on many occasions Sara was told that Susie was too busy playing with her friends to take her calls. In fact on two separate occasions, the Ravenports had lured Sara to their house using the guise of Susie's happiness. Each time her compassion betrayed her as she arrived only to find that Susie was staying over with some friends. This lie had been perpetrated purely for selfish reasons. The real reason for their red-herring was that they were having a dinner party and some of their guests needed a baby-sitter.

After being burnt twice, Sara decided to give them a taste of their own medicine. She showed up one late June day with two tickets to the circus for her and Susie. She found Mr. Ravenport wearing an old stained undershirt, his fat belly bulging underneath as he sat in his chair drinking wine from the bottle. Mrs. Ravenport was still wearing her sack and had curlers in her hair. They weren't exactly your typical millionaires.

"Sara, what are you doing here?" they asked.

"I've come to take Susie to the circus. I bought two tickets," she said with a smile.

"What about us?" they barked selfishly.

"Well, I don't have anymore tickets, so you'll have to buy your own," she chirped.

"No, we're not dressed for it anyway," Mr. Ravenport muttered indignantly.

Sara took Susie to the circus and she had a great time. On the way home, however, Sara was stuck in traffic and was consequently ten minutes late in getting Susie home. Once there, the Ravenports started ranting at Sara.

"You have some nerve," Mrs. Ravenport yelled. "You don't bring her home on time and you have the gall not to buy us tickets after we promised to pay your tuition," she wailed.

"You have no right talking to me as if I'm a child," Sara countered. "I didn't know that the offer to give me the loan came with a catch. If you wanted tickets so badly, why didn't you come with us and buy them yourselves, instead of sulking all night like a pair of spoiled brats?" she hollered storming out of the house. Once again she arrived at my door in tears, relaying the whole sordid ordeal.

The next morning, Sara received a phone call from the Ravenports telling her that they weren't sure if they could give her the $10,000 after all. This devastated her as once again these users who supposedly considered her to be part of their family were proving how they really felt. At this point, she called me crying on the phone.

"Roger," she whimpered. "How could they do this to me?"

Part of me wanted to cry out, "I told you so," while the other wanted to rip the Ravenports' heads off and roll them down the street. Regrettably, I loved Sara and could never tell her I told you so. Also, she needed the Ravenports at that time, since she still remained hopeful that they would honor their promise to pay her tuition in September, when it was due. So, I just stood by and comforted her.

A day later, I was treated to yet another side of her emotional roller coaster.

"Roger," she beamed. "Don't worry about the money, it's all taken care of."

"How?" I asked suspiciously.

"I called April last night and received great news. Apparently one of April's aunts recently was brutally murdered, leaving her with a $12,000 windfall. She promised me that if the Ravenports go back on their word, she will give it to me. Isn't life wonderful?" She laughed.

"Sara, I would not trust her if I were you," I warned her once again. "You can't rely on her, given the fact that she constantly wastes her money on gifts for guys like Jamal," I said somberly.

"Oh, she's matured since Jamal," Sara countered.

"Please," I cried. "How can you say that? Just yesterday you told me that since Jamal there have been five other guys April has given herself to, just to be discarded like a rotten fish," I reminded her.

Sara remained sickeningly optimistic, however, telling me not to worry because even if April failed her, Todd had promised to help.

"How can he help? He can't even take care of himself, never mind his family! How can you possibly expect him to help you?" I shouted literally shaking.

"He told me you'd say that, Roger. You never have faith in anyone. You have to learn to be more trusting. They are my friends, they won't let me down," she screeched angrily.

I didn't even bother responding. What good would it have done, I told myself. She wasn't going to listen and arguing would just upset her. Anyway, she had to learn these people were not worthy of her trust. I wanted her to see them for the slime they really were. Unfortunately, this was going to be a lesson that failed to stick.

Sara spent much of the remaining summer kissing up to the Ravenports. She put up with their lies and mind games by concealing her disdain under a false grin. By the start of August things were starting to look up. After one of their baby-sitting parties, Sara called me bubbling with optimism.

"Roger," she chirped, "everything is going to work out. My efforts have finally paid off. Tonight after the party, the Ravenports called me over and reaffirmed their promise to give me the money when it's due," she stated cheerfully.

"Good for you, Sara," I simply replied.

At the time it seemed a fair tradeoff. A mere summer of false smiles for a lifetime of prosperity. Sadly, we would soon learn that a second cloaked in falsehood is a second too long.

The day after our joyous dinner with Todd and Mary, Sara called the Ravenports to remind them that the semester was approaching, thus she needed them to make good on their promise.

"Don't worry about it sweetie," Mr. Ravenport replied. "We'll have it ready on Monday," he promised.

"A thousand thank yous," she retorted.

"Oh, by the way, Sara; we're having a party on Saturday and wonder if you could baby-sit for us," he asked slyly.

"I'd be delighted to," she replied. Of course this was something she could not refuse. To her surprise, when she went over to get it, they refused to give it to her. When she reminded them of their promise and how she had relied on it, they just laughed. They then had the audacity to promise her that they would have it next year.

It was then that Sara found out what they had wanted all along.

"If you can't afford to go to school, you could always move back with us and be our full time nanny," Mrs. Ravenport chirped.

So this is what they really wanted, Sara thought. They had actually planned it. They didn't care how hard she had worked to become a lawyer or how close she was to accomplishing her goal. All they cared about and all they had ever cared about was themselves. They wanted a slave to watch their child while they wallowed in their own crapulence.

Barbara simply smiled and said, "Look on the bright side of things, sweetie, when I have my baby you can watch her too."

With that, Sara nearly lost it. She wanted to scream out, "Look, you nutcase, you're never going to have a baby because you sterilized yourself! The only thing you'll ever have is a rancid bag of flour!" Wisely she chose not to let them rob her of her dignity. She just stood there calmly biding her time till that glorious day when she would crush them like ants. To add insult to injury, Tim took her aside and told her he had good news.

"I don't want to tell Barbara until it's a done deal, but we're planning to adopt another child which you could watch as well," Mr. Ravenport cackled, as his rhinoceros chin bobbed up and down. "Also as an added bonus, when our children grow up and leave the nest, you can spend the rest of your spinsterhood caring for us in our old age," he said with a smirk.

That night for what seemed like the thousandth time, she came to my door in tears. She couldn't believe they could be so selfish. She finally realized that they had planned this all along. They had never intended to give her a penny. It was all just a scam designed to force her to drop out of law school and become their lifetime slave. Despite their efforts, Sara was determined not to let them win. She still had faith that her other friends would not let her down. She soon found out how wrong she was.

Over the next two days, she left countless messages on April's machine, telling her what had happened and asking for the money April had promised her. Finally, two days before she had to register or drop out, April returned her calls.

"April, where have you been?" Sara cried. "I have been trying to reach you for days."

"Hey, don't yell at me. I have a life to live," April shot back. "It just so happens that one of my old boyfriends was in town for a business meeting. He called me up and told me that he was going to be in town for three days and wanted to see me. At first he told me that he had plans with his friends, so he couldn't go to dinner or a movie, but then he asked me to drop by his hotel room and wait for him to get back."

"April, you didn't?" Sara cried.

"Why not?" April retorted. "You should have seen him, he was so fine. He told me to drop by his room around one a.m. so we could have another slamming night," she giggled. "When he arrived, he gave me a rose and told me how fine I was and I'm not sure but I think the earth actually moved," she joked.

"Oh, April," Sara cried. "Don't you ever learn? This slime comes to town, doesn't want to take you out, yet tells you to wait around his hotel room at one a.m. so he can screw you and you go along. Any woman with a shred of integrity left in her, would tell this slime to go to hell. Yet you go with bells on!" she shouted.

"Oh, that reminds me, I don't have the money anymore," April mumbled quickly.

"What?" Sara screamed. "April, you promised me."

"I know," she replied, "but when I told him about my aunt being murdered and leaving me the money, he asked for it, so I gave it to him."

"You piece of shit!" Sara screamed. "You knew I needed the money."

"Sorry," April replied as she hung up the phone.

So this is what April's word was really worth. This proved that she did not really care about Sara. Anyone who would put the needs of someone who had used and dumped them over the needs of a true friend is not worth crying over. Sara had always been there for April and this was how she thanked her.

Sara's last ditch effort was to call Todd, the last of her supposed friends who had promised they would be there when she needed them. Todd haplessly proved to be nothing more than a lying user. He told her that he would love to help but he was saving his money for a new home entertainment system. He was planning to buy a big screen television and a whole new stereo system. Also he had his eye on a pair of $1500 leather chairs and a $3000 leather couch for him and his friends to lounge on. Sara couldn't believe what she was hearing. This selfish piece of garbage who was getting ready to welcome the ninth member of his own personal cult into the world had lied to her. What made this deception so sickening was its cause. This lie was based solely on self-indulgence. He had stained his soul not because he needed the money to feed his family or to pay his rent, but because he wanted to buy a home entertainment system.

"What do you need a home entertainment system for anyway?" Sara screamed. "That's what I thought you had Mary for!"

"Yeah!" Todd bellowed, "but even I get tired sometimes."

"You selfish piece of shit!" Sara howled. "You know how hard I worked for this, yet you're selling me out for a TV and some chairs!"

"Calm down baby," Todd replied. "Hows about I come over and take you for a ride in my new Jeep?"

With that Sara slammed the phone down and ran to my apartment. So there she was, standing at my door crying her eyes out at two o'clock in the morning.

"What is it, sweetie?" I asked as I held her tightly in my arms.

"Roger, I don't know what to do. They all promised they would help me, but instead they all bailed on me. The school wants my check on Monday or they say I'll have to withdraw from classes. My whole life is ruined!" she cried.

"It's going to be okay, honey; don't worry about it," I told her. "I would never let anything bad happen to you, Sara. You mean everything to me. You know that, don't you?"

"Yeah," she mumbled, "but what can you do about this? They want my check on Monday."

"Well, how much do you need?" I stated bluntly.

"$10,000," she sobbed.

"I'll write you a check then," I replied matter-of-factly.

"You have that type of money, Roger?" she asked amazed.

"Of course I do," I whispered. "You know how I always prepare for the worst case scenario. When I was in college, I worked forty hours a week while taking a full course load, so I could put some money away just in case I needed it during law school."

"How did you manage that?"

"That's one of the benefits of growing up in an abusive household. You learn at an early age how to burn the candle at both ends," I replied with a smile.

"But, what if you need it?" she whimpered, drying her tears on my nightshirt.

"Money does not mean anything to me," I replied. "You know that all I care about is you. If you need something then it's just as if I need it. You're my world and I love you. I would never let anything bad happen to you," I promised her.

"I love you, Roger," she whispered gently.

"I love you too," I replied, tenderly caressing her temples as she quickly fell asleep in my arms.

THE CALM BEFORE THE STORM

That Monday, Sara cashed my check and we began our final year in law school. Later that day she called the Ravenports to tell them the good news.

She told Mr. Ravenports that after much consideration she sadly must decline their generous offer of becoming their house slave. Sara chuckled as she told him that although it had been an agonizing decision to make, in the end she had decided to become a lawyer after all."

Exasperated, he asked, "How could you possibly come up with $10,000 in such a short period of time?"

"Roger gave it to me," she said smiling all the while.

"That's generous of him," he bitterly replied. "Why would he do such a thing?"

"Because he loves me," Sara retorted, beaming so brightly that he could practically see her over the phone.

The next few months proved to be the happiest of my life. For the first time there existed someone I could truly trust or so I thought. We spent almost every day together. Even the days we weren't together were spent on the phone talking endlessly about everything. Although all of her supposed friends had bailed on her when she needed them the most, none of that mattered now since I was there for her.

School was going very well for me. For the first time in my law school career, I was seeing every issue in every case clearly. My moot court performances were very impressive and I received callback interviews from some of the top law firms in the country.

Unfortunately, Sara was not having as easy a time as I was.

This problem had everything to do with her professors and nothing to do with her intelligence. Some of her scumbag professors were actually hitting on her in class. I justifiably call them scumbags because that's what they are. They have a duty to help their students learn the law and are paid amply for it. They have no right to put their own sick sexual pleasures ahead of the best interests of their students. Sara hated this. They would wink at her during class and made sexually explicit comments whenever she would raise her hand.

A few weeks before the end of the fall semester, Sara walked into one of my tax classes and just stood there in tears. While everyone there just gawked happily, glad to see something interesting for once, I quickly took her outside.

"What happened? What's wrong, sweetie?" I asked nervously.

"I want to go home, Roger. Please take me home," she whimpered.

"Sure, anything you say," I replied as I took her home. Once there I calmed her down and she began to tell me what happened.

"Well, I was leaving my ethics class when the professor told me that he wanted to talk to me in his office. Roger, I was so happy," she sobbed. "I thought that he was going to ask me to help him research the *Law Review* article he was writing, but he's no better than all the rest."

"What did he want?" I queried quite angrily.

"He wanted to show me his new foldout couch. He said that he thought I was cute and he wanted me to help break it in. When I told him no, he threatened me," she mumbled, trying not to cry.

"What did he say?" I asked with rage in my eyes.

"He said that if I didn't give him a taste, he'd make sure I'd receive a 'd' in Ethics."

"What did you do?" I asked tentatively.

"What do you think I did, Roger? I told him to fuck off, then ran to you. What am I going to do, Roger? I can't receive a 'd.' This isn't high school where a 'd' can be overcome. You know as well as I do, that a 'd' at this level is a virtual death sentence. Grades are the key determinant in procuring a high paying prestigious job with a top law firm, right out of law school. If he goes through with this, my dream is over," she yelled matter-of-factly. "He knows this and is using it to sow his wild oats."

"Well you'll just have to report him," I said calmly.

"Wake up, Roger. That won't do any good. First of all, he has tenure and is on all the ethics review boards. Who are we going to report him to? Himself," she shouted.

"Well, we will go to the dean then," I countered.

"With what, Roger? That's what he's counting on. That's why he threatened a 'd' instead of an 'f.' Everyone knows that law professors rarely give out 'fs,' but a 'd' won't raise many eyebrows. They'll think I'm just crying over sour grapes."

"All right then, I'll just have a little chat with this ethical pillar of the legal community," I said with a smile.

"No, Roger. I don't want you to get involved," she protested.

"I'm already involved," I replied.

"Just promise me that you won't do anything foolish," she pleaded.

"Forget about it," I stated coyly.

"Roger, promise me that I won't turn on the news, just to see you being led away in chains for disemboweling this piranha," she said sternly.

"Okay, no disemboweling," I said with a smile, as I kissed her gently.

The next few days were spent pondering how to tactfully deal with the situation. I had promised Sara that I would never let anything bad happen to her and I always kept my word.

One late November night, when I knew the professor had a night class so there wouldn't be anyone around his office, I went in and waited for him. His office was covered in Persian rugs and leather upholstery. Upon his marble desk sat a picture of his pretty wife with his young son and daughter. This incensed me. He had been given a lovely wife and two children, yet was throwing it in God's face. As a child, I had foolishly equated education level with wisdom. Unfortunately, having reached the top, I was extremely disappointed. I quickly learned that knowledge alone isn't enough. In order to gain true wisdom you need a conscience. Although knowledge teaches you to look at the big picture, if you only see yourself you'll never truly understand. Education taught men like Todd to keep their composure and cover their asses, yet they remained as selfish as always. While they now understood that their actions had consequences, they only cared about their own personal ends. The fact that lives were ruined because of their actions meant nothing to them.

Hearing someone approaching, I hid behind the door. When he entered the room, I walked out from behind the door and kicked him in an area very dear to his heart. He didn't look like your typical sexual predator. He was thirty-nine years old, about six foot three, and had blue eyes and blond hair.

As he wailed in pain, I grabbed him by the throat and yelled, "This is what happens when you hit on your students, you unethical piece of shit!"

"Which one are you talking about?" he sputtered ignorantly.

"Sara," I yelled back.

"I'm sorry," he whimpered. "I didn't know she had a serious boyfriend."

"That has nothing to do with it," I yelled. "She's your student. Your job is to teach your class the law, not use it as your own personal brothel," I howled. "What kind of an ethics professor are you anyway? Threatening your students with 'ds' if they don't screw you."

"I was just kidding. I never intended to do that," he whined.

"Just shut up and listen," I barked as I held him by the throat. "If you ever say anything that even remotely could make Sara feel uncomfortable again, I will make you my own personal eunuch. You got that!" I roared, as I slammed his head onto his desk, shattering the picture of his happy family, then throwing him to the floor.

"You're through here," he howled rising from the floor. "A few calls from me and your degree won't be worth shit!"

"I don't think so," I countered cheerfully as I pulled a recorder out of my jacket.

"What's that?" he squawked.

"What does it look like?" I said with a smile. "It's a tape recorder and I think the ethics board as well as your wife would be very interested in hearing how you blackmail your students," I coyly replied.

"Maybe we could work something out," he mumbled. "I have many influential friends throughout the legal field. How does a nice $100,000 a year associate position with one of the top firms in the country sound?" he said with a smile.

"No! I don't want it that way," I shot back angrily.

"Oh please, grow up," he countered. "Everything's about who you know. If you're smart, you'll bury that tape and take the job," he bitterly replied.

"No," I repeated vehemently. "If practicing law means selling out Sara, I want none of it. If I reach the top it's going to be because I earned it, otherwise it won't be worth a thing," I replied honestly.

"Well, what do you want then?" he asked perplexed.

"I want you to leave Sara alone, otherwise a copy of this tape will be on the desk of every lawyer in the country along with your wife. You got that!" I bellowed.

"Alright, I got it," he grumbled, trying to wipe the blood from his eyes.

"Good," I stated smugly. "By the way, the same applies if she doesn't get the grade we all know she deserves," I said calmly, as I walked out of the room.

From then on Sara would have no more problems with him. In fact he made sure to keep at least a ten foot distance when answering any questions she would ask. So once again I had kept my promise and taken care of my darling Sara.

The rest of that semester went beautifully. I made sure to take her to all the top movies and shows. I also took her to the most expensive five star restaurants around.

One night over lobster she said, "Roger, you don't have to keep taking me to all these great places. I would love you even if we just went out for pizza."

To this I candidly replied, "Don't be silly, nothing is too good for you, my love."

At that point I was the happiest I would ever be in my life. I had everything I could ever want. Sara was my world. She was the only person who I could truly trust and I loved her for it. I told God that all He had to do was keep things as they were with me and Sara and the past would be forgotten. All He had to do to prove to me that He loved me was give me Sara. Nothing else could ever matter to me.

That December, I watched the plane slowly leave the ground on its way to Paris, totally unaware that our happiness was almost at its end. She had wanted to stay with me during the holidays for she knew how upset my family made me. Alas, I said no, once again putting her happiness above mine. I knew how much she wanted to be with her family, particularly her newborn niece who she had not yet seen. I told her that she should go. I promised her that next year when I was "a big time lawyer," I would take her on the Christmas holiday that she deserved.

"Of course you're right, Roger," she agreed. "That's why I love you. You're always putting my welfare before your own."

This is a day that I shall rue forever. If I had it to do over, I would have taken her to some secluded cabin in the mountains where we could be alone. Regrettably, loving her meant wanting only what was best for her. Therefore, I told her to go see her niece. Never had doing the right thing been so wrong. I never thought that God could be so cruel, that He would take away the one person who He knew meant everything to me. This is what God would want me to do, I thought to myself. This is what eight years of Catholic schooling had taught me. I would soon find out how wrong I was.

INVITE TO OLYMPUS

That year the holidays brought me only pain and misery. The absence from my Sara was particularly unbearable. It was as though some part of me knew something was wrong. I didn't hear from Sara that entire holiday season. This should have served as a warning, just like the calmness of the sea before a storm. The previous Christmas, Sara had called me almost every day. We spent Christmas day on the phone in the kitchens of two houses we did not want to be in, talking the day away. The same went for New Year's Eve. This year would be different. In the three weeks she was away, not a single word did I hear from her, making it the first in a long line of empty meaningless holidays.

After she returned home, I immediately picked up on the change in her demeanor. In the past talking with Sara never failed to bring a smile to my face. Now, that same voice was filled with apathy and avarice, just like everyone else's. This put me into a panic. I could not even begin to fathom my life without Sara in it. To my relief about two weeks after she came home, the warm caring person only I knew and loved returned and life was happy again. It would not remain so for long.

The middle of February brought with it a miserable day. We went to the movies for the first time in almost two months. To make things worse, Sara insisted on seeing one of those tediously predictable natural disaster movies. Afterwards, she begged me to take her to one of those hideous theme restaurants, which the masses so enjoy. At that point, I had to speak my mind.

"What's happened to you?" I asked.

"What do you mean, Roger?" she answered defensively in her shrill lawyer voice.

"There right there," I yelled. "That voice. That's your lawyer voice. Why are you using it on me?"

"I don't know what you're talking about, Roger. What per se is my lawyer's voice?"

"You know, your lawyer's voice," I responded angrily. "That facade you put on whenever you have to go on an interview or law meeting, to protect yourself from the users you will inevitably meet."

"I don't put on a facade," she barked defensively.

"Of course you do. I can always tell simply by the tone of your voice. It changes from that sweet siren song I love so dearly to that harden heartless tone you're using right now," I stated honestly.

"I think you're losing your mind, Roger. The Ravenports have been warning me about you for a while now. Maybe I should start listening."

"See, right there," I yelled. "Why are you still talking to the Ravenports?" I asked, thoroughly frustrated.

"They're my friends," she replied nastily.

"I don't understand you, Sara. I have no idea what's happened to you. Suddenly, you like cliche movies and theme restaurants, things you despised just two months ago. Your voice is cold and heartless almost all the time now and worst of all, you're taking advice from the very scum that previously betrayed you," I howled angrily. "These cretins hurt you, yet you're giving them a second shot at your head. Why?" I roared.

"Stop yelling, Roger," she screamed. "Who I choose to consort with is none of your business. Anyway they're my friends," she stated coldly.

"No, they're not! People who abandon you when you need them most are not your friends!" I howled as she stormed out of the restaurant.

The final months of our last semester proved to be the worst of my law school career. Unlike the previous semester where we spent almost every moment together, this semester we seemed to be growing apart. This would be the first and only time in my life that I would actually be scared. I always considered myself to be very thick skinned. When your father starts beating you at the age of five, it's either develop a strong skin or die. Since then I had not let anyone close enough to hurt me. Sara, however, proved to be the exception. For the first time I let myself become vulnerable by opening up my heart and soul to her. This was a mistake I would never repeat.

For the first time in our relationship we began to fight often. This was destroying me. I hated arguing with someone I adored and didn't want to upset her. Nevertheless, I would rather upset her than permit these vermin to feed.

About a month before Olympus, we had our worst fight yet. We had been seeing less of each other because she claimed that her schoolwork had become very demanding. This I understood. I knew that she had worked very hard and had come way too far just to screw it up now. It was what she did with the little free time she had that actually upset me. In the middle of March, both of us finally had a weekend off. Instead of spending it with me, however, Sara disappeared over the Ides of March.

I left countless messages on her machine, which she coldly ignored. When she finally called me four days later, I totally lost my composure.

"Where were you?" I yelled frantically. "I thought you were rotting in a ditch somewhere."

"I'm fine," she countered in a bitter tone. "I decided to spend the weekend with the Ravenports and spent Sunday night with Todd and Mary."

Her words infuriated me. The very idea that she would rather spend time with them instead of me created feelings of betrayal and rage. "Why would you possibly want to spend the little time you have off with the very people you once considered to be the scum of the earth?" I barked irately.

"Who I spend my time with is none of your business, Roger. You're my boyfriend, not my keeper," she screeched, slamming the phone down.

I could not handle this betrayal. The result was us not speaking to each other for weeks. I spent my nights sitting by the lake searching for a solace that would not come. Three weeks into my sojourn, Sara reemerged from the bushes.

"Well, well, well, look who's here," she sarcastically shouted. "Well, Roger; I believe you owe me an apology."

"What do I have to apologize for?" I asked in disbelief.

"For the nasty way you spoke to me," she angrily replied.

"Your actions justified my tone," I replied honestly.

"Alright, Roger. I'll apologize for worrying you, if you'll apologize for the way you spoke to me."

"Fine," I replied. "I'm sorry I spoke harshly to you," I grudgingly stated.

"And I'm sorry that I worried you," she mechanically replied, with the obligatory embrace.

"How many times must I prove my love to you, before you realize that I would never leave you?" I cried.

"My father claimed to love me as well, but he left," she quickly countered.

"I'm not your father, Sara. I would never abandon you," I whispered gently. "There is no need for you to surround yourself with jackals," I replied.

"I know, Roger, but by surrounding myself with people I'm proving him wrong," she stated emphatically.

"Proving who wrong?" I cried a bit worried.

"My father, Roger. By letting the masses into my life, I'm showing the world that his actions had no effect on me whatsoever, thus assuring myself that I'll never be alone," she shouted.

"But by surrounding yourself with fools you will always be alone and what's worse you're letting him dictate your life," I tried to explain.

"No, I'm not, Roger," she quickly countered. "Living like a hermit would be giving him control. He left me alone, but I'll be damned before I ever let that happen again."

"But you are giving him control. You're practically letting him choose your friends," I shouted.

"Enough, Roger. If you want to be part of my life you'll have to accept my friends," she coldly stated. "Are you capable of doing that?"

"Yes," I replied kissing her gently as we walked home.

That night proved to be a mistake. I had nothing to apologize for, yet I let my fear of losing her cloud my judgement. From then on, our relationship would never be what it once was. Where previously just hearing her voice filled me with pure happiness, now that same voice proved to be a constant reminder of the time she had chosen the users over me.

Nevertheless as upset as I was, I still loved and trusted Sara. In hindsight, I should have foreseen what was about to transpire, yet I shut my eyes to it. I could not believe that my darling Sara, the same woman who I had lovingly held in my arms so many times, would ever do anything to hurt me. I couldn't believe that God would ever be that cruel.

During law school I had worked in the district attorney's office prosecuting sex offenders and wife beaters. I remember being so frustrated as time after time the victims would refuse to testify against their abusers, letting them off the hook. Their reason for doing so was always the same. No matter how badly they had been scarred, they all still claimed to love their attacker. This infuriated me for two reasons, one practical and one selfish. For all practical purposes the old adage of 'once an abuser, always an abuser' proved to be true.

After their attack, the abusers would always apologize and tell their victims that it would never happen again.

Inevitably it always did. Forgiving the abuser only increased the frequency of the abuse. The beatings would go from once a month to once a day, since the abuser no longer feared losing the victim. Eventually the victim would wind up in a pine box. Knowing how things would inevitably end up, yet being forced to stand by inanely watching the body count rise, was one reason why their self-imposed ignorance infuriated me.

A more selfish reason was that I was actually becoming jealous of the abusers. I remember rape trials where the accused rapist just sat and grinned as the poor victim was forced to relive the entire attack on the stand. What made me jealous was the fact that while this was going on, three or four "women," and I use the word loosely, would be standing in the back actually fighting over the rapist. While one arm held Satan's offspring, the other was throwing a punch at their fellow strumpet, evidently in retribution for banging "their man."

Since God allowed this human garbage to still be loved after all he had done to forfeit that right, surely He would not deny me that same privilege. Given the mountain of times I had put Sara's needs above mine, I could not believe that God would take her from me. This belief would be short lived.

In the middle of April, Sara had a surprise for me. Supposedly as a graduation present, the Ravenports had invited Sara to spend Easter weekend at Olympus, their country estate. They told her that she was free to bring whomever she wanted. Of course she asked me to go with her. The date which this fell on proved to be a constant reminder that God knew exactly what He was doing. God was using Easter just to rub my face in it.

I did not want to spend my weekend with the Ravenports. Sadly, once again like a lemming over a cliff I put Sara's wants over mine and agreed to go. As an added bonus, Sara decided to invite April, who being unemployed had nothing better to do. Finally in order to make it just the perfect weekend, she invited Todd and Mary, who was due to give birth any day now.

OLYMPUS

    Olympus was a 50,000 acre estate built on Cape Cod in 1823 by Mr. Ravenport's great grandfather, a giant in the shipbuilding industry. During their lives, his grandfather and father who were industrial and economic trailblazers in their own right, expanded on the estate making it a virtual palace. Upon his death, his father left it to him in his will, along with his brownstone. Originally named Ravenport manor, Mr. Ravenport changed the name upon inheriting it to Olympus, after the supposed home of the Greek Gods.

    Upon seeing it for the first time even I had to be a little impressed. The grounds were massive containing seven flower gardens, two outdoor pools, a hedge maze, a stable and two paths. Following the left path brought you to the ocean, while the right path led to its own small forest. The front of the house was garnished with a long reflection pool, similar to the one at the palace of Versailles. As we drove up to the front gate we saw Todd, Mary, April, the Ravenports, and Susie waiting for us. I didn't trust any of these people and had my suspicions that the Ravenports had an ulterior motive for inviting us up here. Of course Sara told me I was being paranoid and to just enjoy it, but I was not convinced.

    As we got out of the car, we were greeted by Mr. Ravenport who complained that they had been waiting for half an hour and were beginning to get worried.

    "Oh, Roger and I stopped along the cliffs to take in the breathtaking view," Sara explained.

    "Oh, I bet that's all you did," April exclaimed.

    "Now, April, just what are you implying about our Sara?" Mrs. Ravenport chirped.

    "She knows exactly what I'm talking about," April said with a smirk.

"Well, I see you're expecting," Mrs. Ravenport told Mary. "When is the baby due?"

"My boy should be popping out any day now," Todd answered smugly. "I see you have a bundle under that dress, when are you due?" Todd joked staring at Mrs. Ravenport's sack of flour.

"Well, this baby doesn't seem to want to come out," she replied actually believing what she was saying. "Maybe having Mary around will help coax it out," she said with a smile.

"Lets get inside," Mr. Ravenport boomed looking both embarrassed and angry.

"Oh, Tim hates to talk about the baby. By the way he carries on sometimes I think he's jealous of it," Mrs. Ravenport replied jokingly rubbing her sack and talking to it, saying, "isn't that right precious, Daddy's a little jealous."

As we came upon the house we were approached by Hortance, the head butler. The house had a staff of twenty-five servants including Hortance who took care of the manor and supervised the staff.

"Hortance has been here for over fifty years, isn't that right, Hortance?" Mr. Ravenport stated.

"Actually, it's sixty-three, sir," Hortance replied somberly.

"Well, I knew it was something like that; put their bags in their rooms," Mr. Ravenport commanded.

"Yes, sir," Hortance replied. As he left you could tell that Hortance was not amused nor did he seem very fond of Mr. Ravenport. Well, I could understand why. Acting as pompous as ever, Mr. Ravenport beamed as he described the house. The house had four floors and a total of sixty-nine rooms. The west wing of the house faced the ocean, while the east faced the woods. The house had its own wine cellar located deep in the basement, as well as four major banquet rooms.

Although there were twenty-one bedrooms, April insisted on staying with Sara and I. Consequently, this trip was off to a miserable start. We all retired towards our rooms and were told to go to the second floor banquet room for dinner at five. Mr. Ravenport went into the study and quickly slammed the door. On the bottom step of the east wing staircase sat Mrs. Ravenport, holding a doll and talking to her sack of flour.

"See, Mary," Todd said with a snicker, "if you don't pop that boy out soon you're going to wind up just as crazy as that old broad."

"Don't, say that," Sara whispered. "If she hears you she might lose it again."

"What do you mean again?" I asked. "She never touched you, did she?"

"No, Roger, stop being so defensive," she shot back, sharing a long look with April. "Her sister once confronted her about it. She told her that it was just a bag of flour and tried to take it off," Sara told us.

"What did she do?" April asked.

"She stabbed her with a fork," Sara stated matter-of-factly.

"Oh, that's nice," I sarcastically replied. "Not only are they selfish users but they're also nuts."

"Roger, don't start," Sara shot back.

"See, Sara, he's already bossing you," April said with a smirk.

"Roger, calm down, she's just kidding. Go upstairs and start unpacking. April and I are going to the stables," Sara stated.

Walking up the marble staircase towards our room, I wanted to start shooting. I was being replaced by a bag of chips. Adding to my misery, the whiffs of marble in the air created the sensation of having the enamel slowly scraped from my teeth with a rusty potato peeler. Lining the stairwell were small dark stained glass windows, which gave the place an eerie mausoleum feel. Reaching the top, I stopped at a large crimson window and watched Sara and April walk towards the stables. They were whispering and laughing, behaving like a pair of prepubescent school girls.

A somber chill ran up my spine as the solitary demon of distrust began clamoring in my ear. "Begone foul demon," I yelled. "You know nothing about whom you speak."

"Why Roger, don't you trust me?" the demon asked coyly. "Have I not always been right in the past?"

"That was different," I yelled. "They were of your realm. Sara is one of God's creations. She doesn't answer to the selfish beckons of your world. She is kind and loving, thus my faith in her is absolute."

"Oh, is it?" the demon scoffed. "You see how she now looks at you. That gleam of trust is no longer in her eyes."

"Just a passing mood," I countered.

"Oh, you know better than that, Roger," it said with a smile. "You've known since Christmas. You hear it in her voice and see it in her eyes."

"Enough," I screamed. "She loves me! I know she loves me!" I howled.

"Loves you," the demon said mockingly. "You really think she loves you?" It grinned.

"Yes, she loves me," I replied vehemently.

"Oh, really," the demon said with a snicker. "Does she love you like your father loved you? Love you like society loved you? Love you like God loved you? Oh, Roger; have I taught you nothing?" It sighed. "Love is fictitious. It is nothing more than a scam created by greeting card companies and florists alike, designed to fill their pockets. You haven't been taken by their sentimental tripe, have you? Surly, you're smarter than that," it taunted.

"Liar!" I screamed as I ran from the window. So some aspects of her personality had changed. So what! I still loved her, that had not changed. That would never change! I would not let it! God would not let it! Somewhere deep inside dwelled that kind loving soul I had fallen in love with and I would not believe that these sellouts could destroy her. Sara knew I loved her and was too smart to let someone like April change that.

Running into Hortance, I asked where our room was. He told me in the east wing.

"There must be a mistake, we want an ocean view," I barked.

"Oh, no mistake sir, your girlfriend told me that her friend liked the woods and to give them a room in the east wing. She told me that if you wanted I could give you a separate room in the west," he replied.

"No, I'm fine," I proclaimed as I hastily walked down toward the stables. Despite this latest indifference towards my feelings, I still loved her and wanted what she wanted. As I headed down toward the stables, I decided to walk through the woods to clear my head.

Shaded from the sun, it was a dark and mysterious place as giant oaks and weeping willows stood side by side. Most people think the woods are simple and dull, hence the old saying, "If you've seen one tree, you've seen them all." They prefer to label them all as simply trunks and leaves. Once again in their fast food approach to life, the masses have missed the point entirely. Just like the sea, what nature shows you is not necessarily the end all. You can't see what's thriving around its roots, what's scurrying within its trunk or what's dancing high upon its branches. Just because it's easier for the masses to make judgements based solely on appearances does not mean that nature will comply.

As I emerged from the woods, I noticed a small black car sitting on a back road. There arguing loudly with the driver stood Mr. Ravenport. I knew he was up to something, I told myself. He was not the sort of person who would just invite you to his Olympus for nothing. This house was Mr. Ravenport's pride and joy. His tool for creating awe and the mystique of power.

In all her years with the Ravenports, Sara had never been invited here. He usually reserved it to impress his arrogant friends.

So, what was he up to? I knew there was something he wanted and even though Sara was acting so selfishly, I still loved her and was determined to protect her at any cost.

I snooped down behind a bush to get a closer look. There was a woman in the car. She looked to be in her late twenties or early thirties and was yelling at Mr. Ravenport.

"If you don't increase it to $5000 a month, I'm going to expose you for what you did to me," she howled.

From the sound of her voice I detected a Spanish accent but I was not sure from where.

"I'm already paying you $2500 and that's all you're going to get," Mr. Ravenport yelled back.

"I'll be back tomorrow," the woman said angrily, "and if you don't have the money that psychotic wife of yours can just tuck her sack into bed at night!" she screeched.

With that, the woman sped off and Mr. Ravenport kicked at her car, missing it. He then hit a tree and stormed towards the house. So this must be Susie's real mother, I thought. That explains why he didn't want her near his house in the city. Here with all his servants it would be easier to watch her. What I didn't understand was why we were here. What did he need Sara for, I wondered. I ran towards the stables to tell Sara and there they were, smiling and laughing with the stable hands.

"What's going on here?" I yelled.

"Oh, Roger, this is Steve and Will, they were just showing us around," Sara said with a smile.

By the way they both were looking at Sara, I knew that was not all they were trying to do. "I have to talk to you," I said.

"Can't it wait, Roger?" she pouted in a cynical tone, once again sharing a glance with April.

"No, it can't," I said angrily.

"All right, it's almost dinner time anyway. April, are you coming?" she asked.

"No, I'll be in later," April shouted happily.

"I'm sure you will," Sara replied gleaming like a cheshire cat.

So, this was my thanks for being her rock.

"What do you want?" she angrily barked, talking now completely in her lawyer voice.

"What was that?" I yelled.

"Oh, that nothing. April likes Steve and she wanted me to be there to put in a good word," she answered slyly.

"Is that all she wanted?" I asked.

"Roger, if you can't trust me by now then leave," she hollered bitterly.

"I trust you," I replied. "I just don't trust her. Anyway I saw Mr. Ravenport talking with some woman I think may be Susie's real mother," I told her.

"Roger, this is about me. The party is for my graduation, just face it," she barked as we entered the house.

"Why did you ask them for a room facing the woods?" I asked.

"April cannot sleep by the water. The waves keep her up. If you need an ocean view so badly just take one of the other rooms," she answered coldly.

"No, I'm fine," I replied somberly.

I couldn't believe how careless and empty her voice had become. I began to ponder the demon's words. After all it had been right about my father. No, I would not go down that road. That is what it wanted. Sara was the one absolute in my life and I would not let pathetic qualms destroy that.

Arriving at the banquet room, we were greeted by good news. Mary had gone into labor and Todd had driven her to the hospital. Surprisingly, April was not there yet. It was just the Ravenports, Susie, and us.

As we feasted on broiled sole, Mr. Ravenport asked what I thought of the place.

"It is very nice," I told him. "With the ocean on one side and the woods on the other, you must find it to be very peaceful."

"Peaceful, what do you mean peaceful?" he yelled.

"I mean that it is probably a great comfort when you need a place to be alone and think," I replied.

"Olympus, was not meant to be peaceful," he said angrily. "Olympus was meant to hold great parties and to be filled with the clamoring of voices. It is a place for celebrations and a place to bring people when you want to put them in awe of your power," he bellowed. "You can't tell me that you weren't impressed when you came in," he said with a smirk.

"The ocean impresses me," I answered shrewdly. "It must be a great comfort to open up the windows and see the waves crashing against the rocks, as the ocean breeze whips against your bald head."

"Roger!" Sara screamed.

"I'm just saying that it looks like a great place for contemplating your place in the universe and deciding what decisions must be made," I smiled.

"I wouldn't know," he barked back. "I don't have time to waste staring at the ocean."

After dinner Sara and I walked down towards the stables because Sara wanted to go riding. When we reached the stables we could hear moaning coming from the back. We went in and there lying besides a trough was April giving herself to Steve.

"My God, April," Sara giggled. "You just met him two hours ago."

"Yeah, but I knew immediately she was the one," Steve lied.

"Isn't he sweet?" April chirped gazing lovingly at Steve. "Now, get out of here," she yelled.

"All right," Sara said with a smile.

"I hope you know what you're doing," I replied, as we left them to their deep devotions.

"She doesn't learn, does she?" I asked.

"She's in love, what can you do?" Sara said playfully.

"How can she be in love? She doesn't even know the guy," I countered now somewhat annoyed.

"You know April, she falls in love quickly," Sara chirped.

"No, she doesn't," I retorted. "She gets taken quickly, that's all."

"You have to admit, he's mighty fine," she said with a smirk.

"So, what?" I barked. "What does that have to do with anything?"

"You don't understand, Roger, to a lot of people that's everything. Anyway all guys choose us that way, so why shouldn't we do it to them?" she yelled spitefully.

"Because it's selfish and all you're doing is dooming yourself to a meaningless relationship," I countered.

"Well, April, seems happy," Sara shot back.

"Don't bother me then, when he dumps her and she comes crying to you," I said sarcastically.

"You don't know he's going to dump her, they might get married," she stated matter-of-factly.

"Get married! Please, what happened to you?" I shouted. "Six months ago you would have laughed at how childish she's being," I cried mortified.

"Well, maybe I'm maturing," she replied.
"More like regressing," I countered sadly, as we walked back towards the house.

THE FIRST NIGHT

I could not believe what was happening. My beautiful Sara, the one woman who meant anything to me was selling her soul to the devil. Just a few months ago, talking to her made me feel like the ocean in my hair. Now, all she emanated was selfishness and shallowness. Had April pulled what she had just done a few months ago, Sara would have smothered her in a mountain of criticism.

She once told me about a girl she and April knew back in high school in Paris. The girl, I believe her name was Faith, had fallen in love with some guy just to have him cheat on her. When Faith found out about his infidelity she totally lost it and wound up being institutionalized. Sara had used this as a warning to April. Whenever April became despondent after being cheated on by "her man," all Sara had to say was, "Remember what happened to Faith," and April would wake up.

This ability to manipulate the situation when she had to provided me with yet another excuse for loving her. This showed me that she had inner strength and would not be easily swayed by some using pretty boy. Sara was above that, I thought. This was one of the characteristics which made her so special. She knew that looks are fleeting but pure love could conquer all. Now, however, she seemed to be forgetting this and it was destroying me. Sara was the one who was different. In my entire life she was the only person who had ever understood me. Sadly, since returning from Paris she had changed. Much to my chagrin some of the demon's words rang true. Nevertheless, I could not bring myself to believe its grimmest tale. Miraculously on that night my faith in her would be temporarily reaffirmed. For the last time as sort of a tease, God would show me the woman I loved once more.

When we reached the house Mr. Ravenport was leaving for a business meeting or so he said. He asked Sara if she would watch Susie since Mrs. Ravenport was strung out on tranquilizers and Susie didn't know the maids. That night proved to be a horrible tease. April had not returned, so it was just the three of us. This would be the last time I would ever see the old Sara who meant everything to me.

That entire night Sara played with Susie. She told her stories and I watched the two of them as they baked cookies and played puppets. Around ten p.m., Susie fell asleep in Sara's arms as she sang her a bedtime lullaby. For those few hours the Sara I knew and loved was back. I looked into her eyes as she gently rocked Susie to sleep and saw that gentle breathtaking woman who meant everything to me. This proved to be God's cruelest joke. He had taken her from me, just to bring her back for a final farewell. After Sara tucked Susie in her bed and kissed her goodnight, we went back to our room and made love for the last time. Sara fell asleep in my arms that night; however, I stayed awake. I held her as tight as I could, while her heavenly breath caressed my neck for the last time. I dreaded daybreak as I did not want this bliss to end. I figured I had at least three hours before sunrise, but God refused to grant me even that.

Our bliss was ended with the sounds of a door slamming and someone screaming out, "Sara." It was April. She burst through the door and upon seeing Sara lying so peacefully in my arms screamed, "Get away from him, they're all pigs," while throwing her shoe at my head.

Startled, Sara pulled the sheets around herself and asked what was wrong.

"They're all pigs," she repeated, bursting into tears.

"Calm down and tell me what happened," Sara told her, as she put on one of my shirts.

"Steve dumped me," she whined.

"Already?" I asked.

"Shut up!" she shrieked. "You're all alike."

"Hey, don't go comparing me to the jackals you screw," I shouted angrily.

"Roger, she's upset, can't you see that?" Sara yelled. "Now, tell me what he did to you, April," she said calmly.

"Well, we were really happy," April cried. "After you interrupted us, we went back to the cottage behind the house. He told me how beautiful I was and how much he loved me, so I let him have me again and then fell asleep. The next thing I remember was this woman screaming at me and calling me a whore. It was Steve's other girlfriend. I yelled, 'Look, Steve loves me now so get out of here,' and then he hit me.

"He yelled, 'Don't you ever talk to my girl like that you little whore.'

"Crying, I asked him how he could say that after he had told me that he loved me?" she whimpered.

"What did he say?" Sara asked.

"He yelled, 'Shut up, whore. I could never love a little slut like you and I would never tell you that.' Then he turned to his girl and told her that I was a mistake. That he was just lonely and how a little whore like me could never mean anything to him. He then grabbed me by the hair and threw me out the door naked into a ditch; dumping my clothes into a puddle."

"Sara," she cried, "how could he do this to me? I loved him so much and he was so fine."

"Oh, please," I cried sarcastically. "You loved him. You don't even know what the word means. You just went after him because of his looks. That's not love, that's lust," I yelled thoroughly riled by now.

"Roger," Sara shouted. "Don't yell at her. Can't you see how upset she is?"

"Well, it's her own fault," I yelled back. "It's about time someone told her to stop acting like a whore if she doesn't want to be treated like one."

"I don't act like a whore," April cried.

"Of course you do," I replied calmly. "You knew this guy for about two hours and you let him screw you, that's a whore."

"But, he said he loved me," she protested.

"Of course he did," I exclaimed. "He wanted to screw you, what did you expect him to say? He would have said anything to get what he wanted. Any guy who would screw someone he just met is scum, you should know that. Love doesn't have a drive-through window. To really care about someone takes time. You have to get to know them and who they are. You can't love someone you just met. Any feelings he had were feelings of lust not love, there is a big difference and it's about time you learned it. Just because a guy likes the way you look and wants to have his way with you, does not mean that he loves you. It actually has nothing to do with you. It's all about lust. When you lust after something once you get it that's it, but to love something means putting their wants and needs above your own," I stated matter-of-factly.

"Roger," Sara yelled, "she's been through hell, stop picking on her."

"I'm trying to help her," I replied calmly. "Being a friend does not mean just telling someone what they want to hear. If you cared about her at all, you'd stop placating her and just tell her the truth."

"Enough, Roger," Sara yelled.

"No, Sara, he's right," April replied in a low tone. "Steve never loved me, he was just using me as his humping post till his real girlfriend came back. I need to take a shower and wipe the feel of him off me," she muttered.

April went into the shower and Sara helped scrub her until she was almost raw.

"That's enough," Sara told her. "We've scrubbed everything ten times, it's impossible for any of it to still be on you."

"No, I can still feel him," April screamed.

"It's all in your mind. If we scrub anymore you're going to make yourself bleed."

"I know what will do it," April yelled as she ran out of the house.

"Stop," Sara screamed. "Put something on, you're going to catch your death."

We followed her out of the house as she ran towards the stables.

We found her pouring kerosene from one of the lamps all over her body.

"Stop it, you're going to kill yourself," Sara cried.

"No, I have to get him off me. I have to get them all off of me," April shrieked insanely.

With this I grabbed her and took her back into the house, where Sara washed the kerosene off her body. She just sat there muttering to herself as Sara gave her a robe and told her to try to get some sleep. She lay on her bed for five minutes and then got up and went down to the kitchen. I followed her and watched as she put her hands over the on/off knob.

"What are you doing?" I asked.

"I just wanted to make sure it was off," she answered in a daze. She then went back to her bed, lay down for a minute and then did this again. She kept repeating this action over and over for about an hour.

Finally, Sara told her, "Either get some rest or we're going to hold you down until you fall asleep."

"I'm just not tired," she replied. "I need to take a walk."

"Oh, no, you don't," Sara yelled. "Do you think I was born yesterday? I know the minute you get out that door, you will just run back to the stables."

"No, I won't," April cried. "Roger is right. Steve was just a creep and I'm not going to let him get to me ever again. I give you my word on that," she promised. "I just need to take a walk and get some air."

"Alright," Sara conceded, "but don't be too long."

"I won't," she sighed mythically, disappearing into the night.

HOLY SATURDAY

Early the next morning, the Ravenports sent a servant to wake us up and tell us that breakfast was ready. This was not necessary, since Sara had kept me up worrying about April, who had not yet returned.

"She probably slept with him again," I remarked matter-of-factly.

"Oh, Roger, she's not that stupid," Sara replied.

"Oh, please," I countered sarcastically. "It's not like this is the first time she's done this. She pulls this crap all the time, she'll never learn," I scoffed as we reached the dining room.

The Ravenports had already started eating and Susie was still sleeping. Mrs. Ravenport informed us that Mary had given birth to twin girls. Todd told her they would be back later that day.

"Isn't that early considering she just gave birth?" Sara asked.

"Yes," Mrs. Ravenport answered. "I told Todd that they should spend at least three days in the hospital to make sure everything was okay, but he said no. I believe his exact words were, 'I don't have that kind of money to waste on bitches,'" she whispered with a naughty smile.

"That's nice," I replied sarcastically.

"Roger, don't be sarcastic; he's probably just a little upset. You know how much he wanted a boy," Sara explained.

"Why are you friends with that piece of shit?" I asked bluntly. "He's one of the most selfish frauds I've ever had the misfortune of knowing. Usually a parent is jubilant if their child is just born healthy. The only person that matters to Todd is Todd. He doesn't even care about the infants. All he's concerned with is the sex of the child and why do you think that is? Not because he wants a son to carry on the family name as selfish as that is, but because he has this fantasy about siring this super athlete who's going to make him rich and powerful. He should be worrying about how he's going to support his wife and all those children he keeps siring," I proclaimed with disdain.

Sara did not say a word because she knew I was right. She just sat there frowning.

"You're right, Roger," Mrs. Ravenport chirped patting her sack. "The most important thing is that the child is healthy. Tim and I don't care about what our child is going to be. The only thing that matters is that it's healthy. Right, Tim," she said with a smile.

"Yes, dear," Mr. Ravenport muttered in a low voice, looking quite embarrassed.

This delusional babbling was mercifully halted by a barrage of shrill screams emanating from outside. We went to the door and there running towards the house screaming all the while was one of the maids. Mr. Ravenport grabbed her and asked what all the fuss was about. Crying, she managed to mumble that she had gone to the cottage to clean the room and had found a naked woman, covered in blood, lying on the floor.

"Oh my God, April," Sara cried, as she ran towards the cottage. I ran after her, followed by the Ravenports.

"He killed her, I know it," Sara kept screaming as she reached the path to the cottage.

I grabbed her as she reached the door. It was open so in we went. On the floor right by the front door, was the naked body of a woman. It had been badly mutilated and was blanketed in blood. On her chest someone had carved the word whore. Although her face had been badly slashed, we could tell from the roots of her hair that this was not April.

"Do you know who she is?" I asked Mr. Ravenport.

He claimed that he had never seen her before. We called the police and a detective soon arrived. He questioned us all to find out where we were the night before. April and Steve were the only people still not there. Will, the other stable guy, quickly identified the body as Nancy, Steve's girlfriend.

The detective informed us that Steve had a past record of domestic abuse against three other women. In fact on seven previous occasions Nancy had filed complaints against him, just to later refuse to cooperate. Sara was worried that April had run away with this heartthrob. Meanwhile, the police started searching the grounds and began putting up roadblocks in case Steve had not already fled.

"See, I knew something like this would happen," I told Sara.

"It's not her fault. How was she supposed to know?" Sara countered.

"Well, if she actually took two seconds to get to know him instead of giving herself up to every guy who looks her way, she might have known," I replied slyly.

This is something which always disgusted me about April. Superficial women like April never failed to infuriate me. They made their choices solely on fast food reasoning, yet cried when things fell apart. This is one of the reasons I loved Sara. She knew that it's what is in your heart that matters and had not let people like April change her. I never understood how these women could go after a guy "because he looks so fine," and then act shocked when he treated them the same way. They acted as if they expected a relationship founded solely on superficialities to have some deep meaning.

No matter how hard you try to fight it, looks fade with age. Aging is simply God's way of exposing the frauds in life. A relationship built solely on looks was doomed to fade with time. I would never understand how people failed to see this. This was something April refused to see. She like all superficial people closed her eyes to it and said that it would never happen to her. Then when it happened and it always did, she would come crying to Sara, expecting her sympathy.

This was something Sara seemed to understand or so I thought. Given the mountain of heathens who had hit on her in the past just to be swatted away like flies, I considered her to be an expert in ciphering out the users. This is why I refused to heed the demon's words.

DOLLS

Despite the events of that morning, twelve o'clock tea went on as scheduled. As Mrs. Ravenport so poetically put it, "We cannot let what happened to that poor wretched woman ruin a perfectly good tea."

As always, Saturday tea was served in the middle of the rose garden. Mr. Ravenport bragged about how his grandmother's tea parties had been world renowned. During the 1920s, rich tycoons and politicians would flock from all corners of the earth to attend the Ravenports' tea parties. Having seven gardens enabled them to conduct the tea in a different garden every day of the week. Although they no longer held daily tea parties, Mrs. Ravenport still liked to have tea in these gardens.

The set-up was very impressive. There were cast-iron chairs with lace cloths on the tables and umbrellas to shade the sun. There were several types of teas, as well as scones and jams. It was here that I first developed an addiction for scones and raspberry jam. Each table had a floral theme with a different color rose. Ironically, Sara and I were seated at the yellow rose table. On the table sat a crystal vase with one long stem yellow rose. At the end of the tea, Sara took the rose from the vase and handed it to me for safekeeping or so she said. Her plan was to have it pressed into an album when we arrived home. This would never transpire.

We sat at our table enjoying our tea and scones, as Susie sat on the floor playing with her dolls.

"What are they doing?" Sara asked Susie.

"Well, the mommy doll is singing a bedtime lullaby to her little baby girl, while the older sister makes puppets."

"Why is the sister making puppets?" Sara asked.

"Because she likes to play with puppets," Susie answered.

"Shouldn't the sister be practicing her ballet?" Mr. Ravenport asked.

"No, tonight's not her practice night."

"Does she like ballet?" I asked.

"No," she answered quickly.

"Why not?" Mr. Ravenport asked sternly.

"Because, the shoes make her feet bleed."

"Then why doesn't she quit?" Sara asked.

"Because, her mommy and daddy won't let her," she stated honestly.

"Why not?" I asked.

"Because, they like to get all dressed up and show all their friends how their daughter can do ballet," she answered sadly.

At that moment a car pulled up and out came Todd and Mary carrying the twins. Mary's face was covered in black and blues.

"What happened to you?" Sara asked.

"I beat her," Todd grinned.

"Why?" I asked angrily.

"For having bitches," he said with a smile.

"You piece of shit!" I shouted.

"No, Roger," Mary interrupted. "Don't yell at Todd, it's my fault for not thinking boy hard enough," she protested pathetically.

"Damn right," Todd grinned.

"Lets see the babies," Sara cried, trying to break the tension. "They're so adorable. What did you name them?"

"Rose and Julia," Mary replied. "I named them after my grandmothers."

"You must be so happy, Todd," Mrs. Ravenport chirped.

"Why should I be?" Todd answered sarcastically. "It's just two more mouths to feed and what can they do for me, nothing! I wanted a son who would make millions playing basketball and take care of me. What can these two do for me? You take care of them and then they get married and leave you. Good for nothing that's what they are," he yelled irately.

THE CARROT AND THE MULE

Todd looked at Susie and her dolls for a moment and then asked her what she was doing.

"I'm playing dolly," she answered cheerfully.

"Where is the daddy dolly?" Todd asked sternly.

"He's at work," Susie replied in her soft innocent voice.

"See, what did I tell you?" Todd shouted. "What's the mommy doll doing?"

"She's singing to the baby," Susie replied.

"Is the baby a boy or a girl?" he inquired.

"A girl," she said with a smile.

"Are there any brothers or sisters?" he continued.

"Yes, there is one older sister."

"What is the sister doing?" he asked angrily.

"She's playing with her puppets."

"Does the girl win money in competitions?" he yelled.

"No, she just plays with her puppets."

"Well, Susie," Todd bellowed, "if she doesn't make money why should the daddy go to work to support these freeloaders!"

"Todd," Sara shouted. "Stop yelling at her, she's just a child."

"Let her answer my question," he demanded.

"I don't know with that means," Susie replied.

"What means?" Todd blared.

"Freeloader," she mumbled.

"It means someone who doesn't make money and leeches off of others. Why should the daddy pay for his daughter if she doesn't make him money?" he roared.

"Because he loves her," she answered meekly.

"Why should he love her?" Todd exploded, not even looking at her anymore.

"Because, he's her daddy; that's what daddies are supposed to do," she stated matter-of-factly.

"Kids, what do they know?" Todd muttered, glancing at us.

"Well, that's the problem with children," I told him. "It's in their nature to be kind and caring. Selfishness and hatred is something we teach them."

"So, do you have enough kids yet, Todd?" Mr. Ravenport asked, trying to change the subject.

"No," Todd replied adamantly. "I'm not stopping until I have my seven sons and I have six more to go. Mary, you better rest now," Todd yelled. "Tonight, I'm putting another one in your belly and this time you better think boy."

"You have to wait at least five weeks, Todd," Mrs. Ravenport told him.

"Why do you say that?" he asked.

"Well, she can't get pregnant for at least another five weeks. It's biologically impossible and trying could hurt her."

"Oh, great," Todd exclaimed. "Well, you better not complain about the bills this month, Mary, since it's your fault we can't pay them."

The temptation to reach out and strangle this selfish piece of shit was never more alluring. I would never understand it. He had been given the greatest gift a man could ask for, just to snub his nose at it. I think one of the reasons I detested Todd so much was that he reminded me of my father. My father like Todd had also been given a wife who was absolutely in love with him. He then was blessed with seven children. Instead of loving his family, he chose to be envious of others. He would rather have the greeting of a stranger than the respect of his family and in the end he would have neither. Instead of loving his daughters and guiding them towards happy and fulfilling lives, Todd neglected them. He spent all his time and energy on his own selfish desires. I would not be like this.

Every night since I had the privilege of meeting someone as loving and kind as Sara, I had prayed to God for one thing. Each night before I went to sleep, I prayed to Saint Anthony of Padua, the patron saint of miracles. I thanked him for bringing Sara into my life and asked him to keep her well, while always blessing me with her love. This is the only thing I ever wanted. I did not want rich sons like Todd or to be respected by the world. All I wanted was Sara's love. My one request, however, proved too much even for the saint of miracles. The one thing that would make me happy, God refused to grant me. This is why the sight of Todd infuriated me. God had given

THE CARROT AND THE MULE

him a devoted wife and seven children, who he chose to neglect. Was he punished for this? No, he was rewarded with two more daughters.

THE LAST SUPPER

The next twenty-four hours will be forever etched into my mind. It started off with our last dinner. We had planned to leave the next morning, something I was looking forward to. I wanted to get away from this house and all of its jackals. This was just another reward God had given to someone who did not deserve it. The Ravenports had not earned this house from years of hard work. It was the fruit of their relatives' labor. Nevertheless, they had no problem accepting it and showing it off as if they had.

We all sat down to eat dinner that night. The twins were being watched by one of the maids, so Mary was able to join us. Mrs. Ravenport kept up her insane delusions about giving birth to her bag of flour. We all just humored her and smiled. However, a ring of the doorbell would bring an end to our controlled delusions, while setting in motion a landslide of reality destined to bury us all.

The bell's daunting echo was followed by a volley of obscenities as into the banquet room rushed the woman I had seen Mr. Ravenport arguing with the day before.

"Give me my baby," she screamed, looking towards Susie.

"Who are you and what do you want?" Mrs. Ravenport asked.

"I've come to take my daughter back," she said with a smile, walking towards Susie.

"Hortance! Hortance!" Mrs. Ravenport shrieked, as Hortance along with three other servants grabbed the woman.

"Get this woman out of my house," Mr. Ravenport commanded.

"Fine, go ahead, throw me out," she said with a chuckle. "Of course my next stop will be the police station and then everyone will know what you've done."

"Wait," Mr. Ravenport yelled. "Let her go. Now, what do you

want?"

"You know exactly what I want," she barked, "$5000 a month."

"I told you, I don't have that type of money," he replied.

"Please," she countered sarcastically. "Don't insult my intelligence. I may not have all the fancy degrees you and your friends have, but I am not stupid. This house alone could probably keep me quiet for the rest of my life," she said with a smile.

"I would rather die than let this house fall into the hands of a two-bit whore," he bellowed.

"Fine, then I'll just take my daughter and be going."

"Don't you dare lay a hand on my Susie," Mrs. Ravenport yelled. "Tim, who is this foul creature?" she hollered.

"Come on Tim, you heard the lady, tell that stuck-up bitch who I am and what you did! What, did the cat get your tongue? Okay, then, I'll tell it. You see folks, since Tim and lady opium here decided to smoke the night away…"

"Shut up!" Mr. Ravenport interrupted. "You want me to tell them who you are, fine, I'll tell them who you are. She's nothing more than a two-bit whore. When we found out that Barbara and I were sterile…"

"Tim, I'm not sterile. I'm pregnant, see," Mrs. Ravenport interrupted, pointing to her sack.

"Please, Barbara, let me go on."

"Ha, ha, ha, I see lady opium here is a little off her rocker," the woman chuckled.

"Shut up, don't you dare disrespect my wife or I'll drown you in the reflection pool. As I was saying, when we found out we were sterile…"

"Stop, saying that," Mrs. Ravenport yelled. "I'm pregnant, I am."

"No you're not, Barbara. That's just a bag of flour. You know it, I know it and everyone else knows it!" Mr. Ravenport bellowed coldly. Mrs. Ravenport just sat there looking wide-eyed at her husband.

"As I was saying, after we found out we couldn't have children of our own, we decided to adopt. I had heard stories about how a lot of the time the biological mother changes her mind and wants the baby back. Fearing the effect this would have on Barbara, I decided to adopt from another country. I had a business contact in Peru, who knew of this woman who was pregnant and who's parents wanted to sell the baby. Therefore I went down to Peru, paid for Susie and then brought her back here."

"Liar!" the woman yelled. "You make it sound so casual, just like another business deal. Well, it wasn't. First of all my name is Anna Marie and my father used to rent me out as his baby making machine. He and his drunken friends would rape me and then sell the child to greedy Americans like yourself. Although none of this is legal and you know it. That's why you've been paying me $2500 a month, to shut me up. When I raised my price, you ran away to this place. Did you really think I wouldn't find you?" she barked, the dollar signs practically sparkling in her eyes.

"Enough," Mr. Ravenport yelled. "What do you want?"

"You know what I want. $5000 a month."

"I will not be blackmailed by some two-bit whore," he roared indignantly.

"Then I want my baby back and if you don't give her to me, I'm going to the cops," Anna Marie threatened.

"Do you really love her?" Mrs. Ravenport muttered.

"What?" Anna Marie yelled.

"Do you really love her?" Mrs. Ravenport repeated. "If you really love her and promise to take good care of her, I'll give her to you."

"Barbara," Mr. Ravenport yelled, "we're not giving her anything."

"You could have my girls for $4500," Todd shouted.

"No, you're not taking my babies," Mary screamed. "I won't let you," she wailed glaring angrily at Todd for the first time.

"Do I love her?" Anna Marie stated. "Is that what you asked?"

"Yes," Mrs. Ravenport replied. "I want to know how you would treat her if I gave her to you."

"You crazy old bat, you really want to know what I'd do with her. Fine, I'll tell you. If you don't pay me, I'll take her and find someone who will. I don't care if they make her play on some pervert's lap all night long. I have four kids back in Peru and a no good drunken husband. I don't want any more kids. If you're not willing to pay, I'll find someone who is," she replied bitterly.

"Enough," Mrs. Ravenport suddenly shrieked. "Fools, you're all acting like fools. None of you deserve children. Look at yourselves. God blessed you all with a little bundle of joy made of your own flesh and blood to love and teach, but do you deserve it? No!"

"Barbara, calm down," Mr. Ravenport ordered.

"You shut up, just shut up," she howled. "You fool," she screamed at Anna Marie. "You foolish child. You say you have four children at home. With Susie that makes five, yet are you thankful? No! God blessed you with five bundles of joy, but do you appreciate them? No! If I had four children of my own, I'd never let them out of my arms. Not only do you not care about the ones you have at home, but you come up here threatening to take away my only joy. And why would you do such a thing? It's not because you can't take being separated from that little heart which you brought into this world. No. It's because of greed! Pure and simple greed! Not only don't you care about that sweet adorable gift God gave you, but you want to sell her for money! For money!" she wailed irately.

"All the money in the world won't put a baby in my womb. I'm forced to carry this sack, somehow believing that if I wish it hard enough, it will actually become a baby. You want my Susie, you're never going to take my Susie away from me," Mrs. Ravenport howled, running up the stairs. She removed one of the eighteenth century french sabers which had hung as a decoration off the wall and clinched it in her fists.

"Barbara, don't do anything foolish," Mr. Ravenport yelled.

"Shut up you stupid old wind bag. What do you know about foolish? I've carried this sack around for years and now you're telling me not to be foolish. And what about you?" she screamed at Todd. "God blesses you with two beautiful baby girls, but are you happy? No! Look at all the children God has favored you with. How dare you complain. I should come down there right now and put an end to your baby making days."

"Hey lady, what business is it of yours?" Todd began.

"Shut up, you stupid little boy," she shot back.

"Boy, don't call me a boy," Todd yelled. "Can a boy have nine kids? I'm a man!" he howled.

"You're nothing more than an impudent little brat," Mrs. Ravenport wailed sharply. "Being able to sire a child doesn't make you a man. Taking care of your kids and loving them, that's what makes a man. Supporting your wife and making sure your children get the best life has to offer, that's what makes a man. You could have a thousand children, yet you would be no more a man than my Tim here," she blared bitterly.

"That's enough, Barbara," Tim yelled.

"Enough, oh no my dear loving husband, I am just getting started. Look at the both of you. You're both spoiled little brats. Look at him," she shrieked, pointing at Todd. "That's no man. A man provides for his family. A man doesn't expect his children to provide for him. I hope your son does make a million dollars and doesn't give you a penny of it."

"Don't you dare smile," she screamed at Mary. "I should take this blade and slit both of the throats of those little angels of yours. I'd be doing them a favor."

"No," Mary screamed. "Stay away from my babies."

"Why?" Mrs. Ravenport replied. "So they can grow up in poverty, hated by their father. Is that the life you want for your children? What kind of a mother are you?" she uttered loudly. "You can't even take care of the children you have, but what do you do? You go and have more with that piece of crap," she yelled pointing at Todd. "The boy treats you like garbage, cheats on you, and spends all your money on cars and hookers. Do you leave him? No! You just bring more children into this world to be abused and tossed aside. You're no more a mother than I am," she shrieked, grabbing at her sack.

"Barbara, just calm down now," Mr. Ravenport yelled. "You don't want to make a scene."

"Oh no, we wouldn't want that now, would we? That would be embarrassing. What would all those stuck up, arrogant, so-called friends of ours say? I can hear them talking now. 'Did you hear about that poor sap Tim Ravenport? He can't even control his own wife. What a disgrace he is to the name Ravenport,'" she mimicked.

"Come down here right now or else!" Mr. Ravenport commanded.

"Or else what, Timmy? What are you going to do, divorce me? Think of what people would say. How your grandfather controlled a family of thirty as well as being a captain of industry, while you couldn't even control one little woman."

"That's quite enough now," Mr. Ravenport shouted.

"Oh, no, I'm not finished yet, my darling husband. I'm through taking orders from you. When we got married, all my friends were so envious of me. They all wanted to know how it felt to be part of the great Ravenport clan. They all wished it was them going to all the parties and holding all of the gala balls. You know what, I wish it was them too."

"You ungrateful little wench," Mr. Ravenport roared. "After all I've given you, this is how you repay me. I made you a queen. You say your friends were jealous, well they should have been. I made you a Ravenport! I gave you more money and power than most people could dream of and this is the thanks I get," he thundered.

"Repay you, I should kill you," Mrs. Ravenport howled. "Had I known the true cost of being Mrs. Ravenport, I never would have done it. Sure there was money and parties, so what. I had the joy of playing hostess to a bunch of arrogant snobs, while you rubbed their noses in all we had and they hated me for it. The price! You want to know the price! The price was my soul! I always had to keep up with the trends. God forbid we read the wrong novel or ate in the wrong restaurant. I made sure we always did "the in thing," and what did it do for me? It made me barren and you sterile as a mule. I never wanted to take LSD, but it was the sixties and everyone was doing it. Alas, everyone doesn't have to wear this stupid sack and call it their child. That's what it's given me; but do you care? No! All you care about is what those arrogant snobs will think. That's why you went to Peru to get Susie. You didn't want a reminder that you had to buy a child.

"That's why we're here tonight, not because of Sara's graduation.

That's right," she said looking straight at Sara. "Do you really think we care about the graduation of one of our servants? Oh, don't look so hurt. Don't tell me you actually believed that we cared about you. For god sakes, we went out of our way to make sure you didn't have the money for school so you would drop out and wait on us."

"But, why?" Sara cried utterly dejected. "Why not just hire another nanny? Why try to ruin my life?"

"It was the principle of the matter," Mrs. Ravenport stated matter-of-factly. "You were our pet project. Our very own 'Liza Doolittle.' We paid for your college, provided you with food and shelter, and introduced you to high society. In short, we owned you. You were supposed to be our entertainment. The star attraction at our parties. It wasn't up to you to leave. It was strictly our call. It would have worked too, if Roger here hadn't butted in. Him we hadn't counted on. After all, who would have thought that anyone would actually love you, given the parade of pretty boys who passed through your bed. Did you really think that any of them cared about you? Even you're not that stupid. Then again, maybe you are. After all, you thought this weekend was about you," she said with a smirk.

"This weekend was about Tim. I see it all clearly now. He didn't want Anna Marie causing a commotion in front of his precious friends, so he met her out here where no one would know. You don't even care about Susie. All this was just to make sure that no one found out how pathetic you are," she yelled, pointing her saber at Tim. "Well, I don't care who finds out. I'm not going to let anyone take my Susie from me," she howled, charging at Anna Marie with her saber drawn.

As she lunged towards her, she slipped and came tumbling down the stairs. The saber flew from her hand as she hit the floor, while her sack of flour burst, creating a virtual cloud. When the air cleared, Mrs. Ravenport was lying in a pool of blood on the bottom step and Anna Marie was pinned against the wall. The blade had skipped through the air finding its mark, landing smack right in the middle of Anna Marie's throat. It tore completely through it, splitting her larynx and coming out the other end. It had practically pinned her to the wall, directly below a picture of Louis the Sixteenth. Her short miserable existence had finally come to an end.

We ran towards Mrs. Ravenport. She was lying face down in a puddle of blood and flour. Susie picked up her head crying, "Mommy are you alright?"

Upon seeing her face, she ran to Sara, shrieking, "She's a clown, she's a clown."

Her face had been blanketed in flour, her blood trickled down it. She was no more. Inevitably consumed by the reality of what she had become.

ORPHANS

Their deaths proved a mere prelude of things to come. Sara was comforting Susie, when Todd asked if he could talk to her alone in our room. Hearing this I followed them to the room and listened at the door.

"What is it?" Sara asked.

"How would you like to give me a son?" Todd laughed.

"What?" she replied, totally flabbergasted.

"You heard me. How's about giving me that son?" he said with a smirk.

"This is not the time to be joking around," Sara answered in an aggravated tone.

"Who's joking? I'm dead serious," Todd laughed pushing her onto the bed, at which point Sara screamed and I burst into the room.

"Get the hell off her," I yelled running towards him.

He yanked Sara up by her hair and pulling a knife from his belt, held it to her throat yelling, "Stop right there or I'll put an end to princess here," at which point I froze.

I had no idea what to do. I wanted to rip his face off, but she'd be dead before I reached him.

"Todd, stop this foolishness right now and let me go," Sara pleaded in a quivering tone.

"But then you'd miss all the fun I have in store for you," he said smiling brazenly.

"What fun?" Sara asked nervously.

"Why I told you, I'm going to put my baby in your belly and you better think boy, bitch," Todd grinned.

"You're going to have to kill me first," I shouted.

"What's the matter, Roger?" Todd laughed. "You never heard of sharing? You had your chance, now it's my turn," he chuckled.

"Todd, I'm your friend, how can you do this to me? Think of how upset Mary would be," Sara pleaded.

"Oh, please." Todd laughed. "You really think we're friends? You've been plan B since the day I met you."

"What does that mean?" Sara shouted. "What the hell is plan B?"

"You know, plan B as in boy. If Mary couldn't give me all my sons, you were my next stop," Todd stated matter-of-factly.

"So, you never really cared about me. All the times you said that you would be there for me, those were just lies?" Sara asked angrily.

"Well, I had to tell you something to make sure you'd be there if I needed you. Don't look so upset, sunshine," he said with a smile. "You should be honored that out of all the women in the world, I chose you after Mary. Anyway, you're going to enjoy this."

"It's never going to happen," I yelled. "You're living in a dream world, Todd. Now let her go," I bellowed.

"Don't tell me what is going to happen," he yelled angrily. "I'll tell you what is going to happen, Mr. big time lawyer. You're going to go out that door the same way you came in," he ordered. "Don't worry," he grinned. "You're not going to lose her. After I'm done with her, you can be there to help her through the morning sickness."

"That's not going to happen," I yelled back.

"Well, if you want to see little Sara here alive again, you will do exactly what I said," he countered.

"You would actually kill me?" Sara asked, the rage beginning to burn in her eyes.

"Hey, it's nothing personal, baby; you're just my means to an end. Anyway, it's all up to Roger here," Todd stated still grinning.

"No, it's not," Mary screamed, as she came in holding a bloody Saber.

"Mary, where did you get that thing?" Todd yelled.

"I borrowed it from Anna-Marie, she didn't seem to need it any more," Mary cackled.

"Mary, get out of here right now or I'm going to hit you so hard, you're going to wish you were never born," Todd yelled.

"I don't think so," Mary shrieked. "You're never going to touch me or any of our kids ever again. You got that?" Mary yelled, pointing the blade at him.

"Don't you point that thing at me, bitch," Todd shot back. Then noticing the look in her eyes, Todd quickly changed his tone of voice. "Mary, sweetheart; what is it? Is it Sara? Come on baby, you know she doesn't mean anything to me. You're the one I love. That's why I'm doing this. This is all for you," he said with a smile.

"What do you mean?" Mary asked looking puzzled.

"I know how hard having the twins was on you and I didn't want to put you through that again. That's what Sara here is for. I'm just using her to have my sons, then you and I can raise them. She means absolutely nothing to me. She's just an oven to cook the bread in. Okay, honey; now put down the blade and wait outside, alright."

"No, not alright," Mary howled. "How stupid do you think I am?"

"What do you mean?" Todd asked meekly.

"You know exactly what I mean. How stupid must you think I am, that I would actually believe you were doing this for me. You've never done anything for me. It's always been about you. All the kids, they are just your way of avoiding responsibility. It has nothing to do with me or with Sara. It's all just about feeding your monster ego. The superstar son who was going to give you millions. That's just a fantasy of yours. A pipe dream in which you could get rich without actually working, while in the process creating a living tribute to Todd. It's always been about you. Your wife, your children, none of this means anything to you. You'd rather live in a dream world than deal with reality. Mrs. Ravenport was right. You're not a man, you're just a spoiled little boy."

"Shut up," Todd yelled angrily.

"Or what, Todd?" Mary yelled back. "What are you going to do, hit me again? No, I'm never going to let you hurt me or our children again," she howled.

"Well, then," Todd replied smiling insanely. "I guess I'm going to have to cut my brand into your face, so you'll remember who the boss around here is," he yelled, throwing Sara to the floor and pointing his knife at Mary.

"Don't come any closer, Todd," Mary screamed. "I'm warning you. If you come one step closer, I'm going to have to hurt you."

"You, hurt me!" Todd laughed. "You can't hurt me! No one can hurt me! I'm invincible!" he roared, lunging at her with his knife.

Mary pulled her saber back and then thrust it forward, right into his groin.

"Ah!" Todd wailed, falling to the floor. "You witch, what have you done to me?"

"I've put an end to your baby making days and now I'm going to put an end to you," she said with a rye smile, pulling the saber out of his groin and lifting it high into the air. "Bye, lover," she chirped, plunging the saber down into his chest as hard as she could, ripping his heart in half, killing him instantly.

With that, the police who had been called came running into the room. Mary just stood over him, still attempting to plunge the saber even deeper into his chest.

"Let go of the blade, ma'am," the officer yelled, grabbing her. It took three of them just to pry her hands from the saber. Todd's lifeless body just lay there, pinned to the floor.

"We're going to need all of you to come down to the station with us, so we can sort this whole thing out," the officer told us. After they cuffed her and were taking her out of the room, Mary screamed, "What about my babies?"

"What babies?" the officer asked.

"They have twin girls in the other room," Sara told him.

"Do they have any other kids?" the officer inquired.

"They have seven more who are staying with their sitter," Sara replied.

"I'll call child welfare to come get the twins," the officer stated. Then he asked Sara to write down Mary's baby-sitter's address so child welfare could take them as well.

As we went down the stairs, the chalk outline people were working around the bodies of Mrs. Ravenport and Anna Marie. Reporters flocked around Mr. Ravenport and Susie as they were led towards the police car.

I found it amusing that Mr. Ravenport had brought us here to protect himself from one scandal and in doing so created a far bigger one. As they entered the police car, Susie saw Sara and cried out for her to come with them. Not wanting to cause the poor girl any more anguish, she agreed to go with her. She told me that she'd meet me at the police station. I watched as she entered the vehicle and it drove away disappearing into the night. Little did I know that the Sara I loved so deeply would disappear with it.

EASTER SUNDAY

    I arrived at the police precinct a little after midnight. It was Easter morning. I looked around the waiting room for Sara, but did not see her. I asked the desk sergeant if she had seen her and was told that she was in with the detectives. I asked her to tell Sara to wait for me if she finished before I did and she agreed. An officer brought me to an empty room, where I was told a detective would be with me shortly. It was three hours until he finally arrived. After answering his questions concerning the events of that evening, I was informed that Mary had given a full confession. They then asked me some follow-up questions concerning her state of mind. When they finally told me I could go, it was 6:30 a.m. I looked around for Sara but was told that she had left hours ago. On the way back to the house, I came upon a small stone chapel and decided to go in. The seven o'clock mass had just begun, so I decided to stay for it.
    This was the first time I had been in a church in over ten years. My past experiences with church and God had not been pleasant ones. As a child I had vivid memories of my father cursing and beating me, because he did not want to be late for mass. Not that we ever were late. In reality we were always an hour early. I guess beating me was just a way he dealt with his stress.
    I remember that the pastor of our church answered to a golden master. Although he knew that many of his members were abusive towards their wives and children, their contributions silenced him. I never thought much of church. The rats would scurry in, recite their devotion to God and then scurry back to their wicked ways. I'd watch these hypocrites lift the chalice to their lips, hoping to see them melt away, only to be disappointed. My childhood prayers had always gone unanswered. I prayed that my father would love me instead of

beating me; it never happened. I prayed for my grandmother's health, just to have her die the next day. Nevertheless, I still believed that God loved me. Consequently, I always wore the gold crucifix my grandmother had given me as a child around my neck.

For some reason that Easter I went into the chapel and sat in a pew. I was taken by the beauty of this chapel, as it looked nothing like my childhood church. Virtually the entire inside of the chapel was covered in lustrous Italian marble. There was a golden chalice and six long stained-glass windows along the sides of the chapel. I could practically smell the holiness in the air.

For some strange reason that moment, I was filled with absolute confidence that God loved me and would honor my prayers. I had but only one prayer. It was the same prayer that I reiterated every night. I prayed that God keep my Sara safe and healthy and let us always be together.

"Surely, God could not be so cruel and hate me so much, that He would take her from me," I pondered positively. God knew that she was the only person who made me feel as happy as I did when the ocean breeze blew through my hair. At the end of the service, I dipped my cross in the marble holy water dish. As I did this, I repeated my prayer. Once again my prayers would go unanswered.

As I walked along the cobblestone road towards Olympus, I was blanketed in a picture perfect day. The sun was shining, the birds were singing, and the sky was blue. It was the most pristine day I had ever seen, perhaps too pristine. I should have noticed that I was being set up, yet I had banned the demon of distrust from my thoughts. That day my mind was on one thing and one thing only. I wanted to see my lovely Sara. As I walked up the road towards the house, I spotted a flashy red car in the driveway but thought nothing of it. After all, given the events of the previous night, it could have been anyone's car.

Before I saw Sara, I wanted to get her a present for Easter. I wanted to show her that although many of her so-called friends had abandoned her the night before, I was still there. I wanted her to know that I still loved her and would always be there for her. I remembered the flower gardens and headed towards the lily garden. There in a tiny grove next to a rippling creek were the Easter lilies. I carefully picked the best twelve of the lot and held them together as a bouquet. I then headed towards the house to give them to my love.

When I reached the house, Hortance told me that Sara was with a friend down by the stables. As I headed towards the stables, I wondered who this could be. The only person left I knew of was April, so I figured maybe she had returned. As I entered the stables, I heard heavy breathing coming from within. I rushed in and found to my utmost horror, my loving trustworthy Sara being mounted by some buxom buck. My gut reaction was disbelief. I wrapped the lilies around his neck and used them as a harness to drag him off her.

"Roger," Sara screamed, for the first time noticing me as I continued to choke the life from him.

"Get off of him," she yelled.

"But he was attacking you," I muttered with a stunned look on my face. I had forced myself to believe the lie that this was actually an attacker.

"No, he wasn't; we were making love," Sara cried.

I let go of my grip, as his head and the lilies hit the floor. I just stood there staring at her as my heart exploded inside my chest.

"This is my friend, Beau," she tried to explain. "He was my boyfriend before I met you, Roger. He left me for a job in South America, three years ago, but recently received a better offer here."

I made no movement, I couldn't. I felt as if I had died but awoke in time for the autopsy. "How could you do this to me, Sara?" I managed to mumble.

"I'm not doing anything to you, Roger. It's not like I planned this. Beau just showed up this morning with red roses. He told me he loved me and all the old feelings came rushing back."

"So, you've been lying to me then," I stated dejectedly.

"No, I haven't, Roger. How could I lie to you if I never told you about him?" she said with a smirk.

"I mean when you said you loved me. Was that all a lie?" I asked pathetically.

"No, it wasn't," she shot back defensively. "I meant it then, it's just that I love Beau more."

"You mean to tell me that after all I've done for you, this is how it ends. So, this is the thanks I get for the countless times I dried your tears and stuck by you when everyone else abandoned you? You would betray me, someone who has proven his love for you time and time again, for this," I yelled pointing my finger at Beau. "A guy who left you for a job!"

"Come on now, the lady's made her choice, it's time for you to vamoose," Beau cackled vilely, attempting to push me away with his hand.

Enraged, I grabbed a shovel lying against the trough and lifted it up like a bat. Then turning to Beau, I yelled perhaps louder than I had ever yelled before, "If you ever touch me again, I'll make sure your death is slow and painful."

"Are you threatening me?" he asked.

"No," I replied calmly. "I'm making you a promise and unlike Sara here, I never go back on my word." With that, I threw down the shovel, kicked the battered lilies lying on the floor, and stormed out of the stables.

I went up to the house, grabbed my bag and threw open the door slamming it behind me. I could not believe that she would do this to me. I could not believe that God would do this to me. As I headed down the steps, Sara and Beau, now fully clothed, came up the walkway.

"Roger," she chided, "you're being childish about this."

"Oh, really." I laughed quite insanely. "I guess I never learned the proper etiquette on how to act when the love of your life betrays you," I bellowed, staring directly into her eyes.

"Please, Roger; you know I need more than just you. I need to make people envious of me. Beau here likes to go to clubs and everyone there thinks he's so fine. I need that. I need all these people and you always hate them."

"That's because they are always trying to use you," I yelled in utter disbelief.

"See, that's the problem, Roger. It's my choice who I let into my world and you can't accept that," she stammered, attempting to put the blame on me.

"That's because I love you and don't want anyone to hurt you," I gasped weakly. "You can't expect me to just sit back and watch quietly, while you let the same users repeatedly burn you."

"Well, it's my life and I'll determine who I let in. If I want to surround myself with users, that's my choice. I'm a big girl, no one's going to make me do something if I don't want to. Anyway, I'm smarter than them. I can be just as phoney as they can be and they will never know," she stated matter-of-factly.

"Sara, you can't surround yourself with liars and users and not expect it to effect you. You may be gaining a lot of user friends but think of the cost," I pleaded.

"What cost? There is no cost," she replied smugly.

"Have I taught you nothing?" I muttered sadly. "Everything always has a cost. Did you learn nothing from yesterday? If you surround yourself with liars and users, pretty soon you won't be able to distinguish yourself from them. You will lose everything that makes you special, everything that I love about you. Your kind nature, the inability to abandon people. To live in their world means suppressing that nature," I tried to explain.

"So, I can do that," she said with a laugh.

"Yes, but by suppressing everything that makes you different, you will become like them and soon enough you will be them. Do you see the cost?" I cried.

"No, what is the cost?" she said with a snicker.

"The cost is your soul, Sara. Those weeds are threatened by you because your nature exposes them for what they are. Thus, they must destroy that flower of virtue which thrives within you. By surrounding yourself with them, you're allowing them to slowly sap the life from that flower. If you let this continue, soon you'll be nothing more than a rotten stem on the ash heap of life," I tried to explain.

"Oh, Roger," she chuckled. "You're so melodramatic. The fact that you can't cope with other people doesn't mean that I can't. That's why I'm going back with Beau. He's an expert at fitting right in," she said with a rye smile.

"That's because he's one of them," I yelled. "Do you really believe that someone who determined that a job was more important than you, could actually ever love you the way I do? You can't be that stupid," I cried.

"Don't you dare call me stupid," she barked. "Just because Beau's life doesn't revolve around me, doesn't mean that he loves me any less. After all I can't expect him to put his job above me, that would be selfish."

"No, it isn't," I yelled. "That's what love is. Love means forever putting the other person's needs above your own wants. If he really loved you, he wouldn't be able to picture life without you and would never put anything ahead of you. That's how you know you love someone.

"Don't you remember all the fancy restaurants I took you to? How I paid for your school and rent. Do you remember the night you told me, 'Roger, you don't have to do this,' and I answered, "'Yes, I do'?"

"Yes," she replied.

"Do you know why I had to? It was because I loved you. That meant that your concerns and needs came above my own and nothing could change that. I told you how much you meant to me. How you meant so much more to me than money and that I would do anything for you. That's true love. This guy doesn't love you. For god sakes, Sara, he left you for a job, and look at the type of job it was. He wasn't leaving to find a cure for cancer or for some other noble cause. He left you for money. He left because he could make a few more bucks there than here and he only came back because the pay was higher. That's not love. Surely, you can see that," I pleaded.

"Enough, Roger," she yelled. "Beau, do you love me?"

"Yes," he replied grinning from ear to ear.

I had seen that grin before. It was the grin of the rapist.

"That's good enough for me, Roger," she said with a smile. "Anyway, look at him; he's gorgeous. He will make everyone jealous."

"So, that's it. In the end, you're just as superficial as everyone else. Well, I have a little secret for you. You've now become April. Well, enjoy it while you can, because there is one thing you and I both know always destroys superficial relationships," I replied slyly.

"What is that?" she said with a smirk.

"Time," I replied. "No matter how hard you fight it, time will always catch up to you. I'd give you at the most seven years, until Beau here finds someone who's younger and tighter and drops you in a heartbeat. Then you will have the rest of your life to ponder alone what you gave up. I would have stayed with you forever and treated you like a queen. You chose style over substance, so now you have to live with it. I hope you know what you're doing," I stated sadly.

"Oh, I know what I'm doing, Roger," she said with a smile. "You're not blind. Even you can see what a beautiful couple we make. Everyone is going to be so jealous of me. Even our reflection is beautiful," she replied as they walked up to the reflection pool hand in hand. "See," she gloated, looking down into it.

The murky air of smugness was suddenly pierced by Sara's shrill scream as she fainted face first into the pool. Upon hitting the water, she awoke to find herself face-to-face with April, her eye hanging out of its socket.

"Ah!" she screamed hysterically as I pulled her out. Looking down into the pool, we could see April's rotting corpse, lying just below the surface.

The police were called and once again, "Olympus" became a media Mecca. The police began pulling her body out of the pool, but her legs seemed to be stuck to something. When they pulled harder, the rotting corpse of Steve came bobbing to the surface and then sunk back down. Eventually, the police were able to remove both bodies from the pool.

Steve had duct tape over his mouth. On his chest the word liar had been carved. When they removed the duct tape, they found something lodged down his throat. It was this obstruction which had prevented him from breathing, causing his death. They reached down and removed the obstruction. It was his genitals. April had cut them off and shoved them down his throat, suffocating him. She had also carved the word liar on his chest.

Later tests would find Nancy's blood also embedded into April's clothing, suggesting that she had killed them both. The coroner would find her death to be a suicide. After killing Nancy, she eventually killed Steve and dumped his body in the reflection pool. She then drowned herself. This explained why Steve's body was behind hers. Once again the police questioned everyone and once again, "Olympus" made the headlines and became infamous for its gruesome murders.

As I left Olympus for the final time, I saw Mr. Ravenport just sitting in the banquet room, staring vacantly at the chalk outlines. On his lap sat his glasses, their purpose now moot. I walked out the front door and went up to the reflection pool. I looked down into it and saw myself. My eyes were sad and hollow. Everything that mattered had been taken from me. I gently removed the crucifix from my neck for the first time since my grandmother had given it to me.

I remembered her telling me, "Roger, as long as you wear this, God will never let anything bad happen to you."

I dropped the crucifix into my hand and gazed at it for a moment. I then grasped it in my fist, pulled my arm back as if throwing a baseball and threw it high into the air. I watched as it disappeared into the middle of the pool with barely a ripple.

Less than a second later, the pool was back to its old seductive self, acting as if its newest acquisition had never existed. Impervious to this latest indignity, I got into my car and drove home.

THE WALKING CORPSE

The next couple of months were a blur to me. I could not accept and was not ready to deal with the magnitude of their betrayal. When I say their betrayal, I am talking about both Sara and God. I had prayed for almost three years now, every single night, thanking God for Sara and begging that He never take her from me.

I had never been a very trusting person. I guess that has to do with the abusive father. There are three people you should always be able to trust in this world; your mother, your father and God. The only souls who I had ever really trusted were my grandmother, God and Sara. Now I had nothing.

My life felt utterly meaningless. I tried to fill the void and quench the pain by drinking and drinking heavily. Over the next couple of months my diet consisted mainly of Merlot, Bordeaux, Chardonnay, and any other French made wine I could get my hands on. It had to be made in France, however, no other wine would do. Upon reflection it's ironic that the very poison I had used to forget her would remind me of her. My days were spent sitting in class, something which proved to be an exercise in futility. While my body was there, my mind was not. Everything reminded me of Sara and what she had done. My concentration as well as my will to live were both gone. I would spend eight or nine hours a day sitting in class trying to hold back the tears, just to come home to an evening of drinking, sobbing and cursing at God. As an added bonus my insomnia had returned.

The worst thing about insomnia is feeling totally exhausted while knowing there will be no relief. A common misnomer about insomnia by those not cursed with it is that those inflicted with it do not become tired or exhausted. It is often looked upon as a blessing, enabling someone to undertake vast amounts of work without succumbing to exhaustion. Nothing is further from the truth. Insomnia brings with it a feeling of eternal exhaustion. The tormented forever dangle within view of the summit, doomed to never reach it. The masses at this point close their eyes, shutting off their proverbial on switch and allowing their bodies to rest. Sadly, the insomniac's switch is broken and cannot be turned off. The insomniac is forced to lie there unable to rest, each night becoming more and more exhausted with no relief in sight.

My first battle with this beast took place shortly after my first childhood beating. These battles would continue to plague me well into my adult years. I had used every type of sleeping pill available, but they only proved a tease. They would work for a day or two and then become useless.

In Sara, I had found a cure for my insomnia, or so I thought. Shortly after I began to trust her, my insomnia had ceased to plague me. In retrospect it makes perfect sense. My trust in Sara filled the void that the beatings had created. When you can go to bed, safe in the presumption that there is someone who loves you and would never betray you, it is a lot easier to sleep.

Now, however, this presumption had been destroyed, for not only had I lost Sara but I had also lost God. I no longer could fake myself into believing God cared about me. When God allowed Sara to leave me, all faith in Him vanished forever. With noone left to trust in this world, my insomnia returned stronger than ever. I would go weeks with no more than an hour or two of sleep. The little sleep that I did have was filled with vivid and often violent flashbacks of the betrayal. Soon all the wine in France ceased to protect me from my memories. My life became a living nightmare. A series of bleak days filled with nothing but self-loathing ensued.

Where previously my skills as an attorney had been highly sought after, now that interest started to dwindle. I would go on interview after interview, depressed and angry and it obviously showed. My mail became a pile of form letters, thanking me for my interest in their firms and conveying their best wishes on my future endeavors. This in itself is usually enough to drive a law student to suicide. You exhaust yourself working for three years, wrecking your vision and giving yourself ulcers. This is all done in the hope of obtaining a $100,000 a year job, only to find out that it was all for nothing.

Oddly enough, I did not care. All the rejection letters in the world meant nothing to me. I had made Sara into my world. Never had I met such a strong-willed and brilliant person, who also was kind-hearted and loving. Law school, future jobs, the loans I had to repay, none of this mattered to me.

As final exams approached, I was faced with a harrowing task. Surviving exam month is difficult when you care. When you don't, it's almost impossible. To truly understand the ordeal of law exams, you have to experience it for yourself. You spend months briefing case after case and reading hundreds of pages nightly. You are then asked to remember and correctly apply every rule in the subject area. The only way to familiarize yourself to the point of being able to do this, is to spend exam month as it's called in the library.

Exam month consisted of waking up and going to the library, where you sat trying to stick every bit of information in your head. Often this meant spending every waking hour sitting there in silence, reviewing material so tedious that it made the most menial empty task seem enjoyable in comparison. This had to be done every day. The only break you had was the four or five hours you received to actually take the exam. Finishing an exam meant putting away one set of torture and picking up another.

After two weeks, fighting off madness became a challenge. The only thing that had gotten me through this in the past was the knowledge that I was doing this for Sara. To be able to give her the life she deserved, I had to do well.

In the past this had been a joint effort. Sara sat across from me and we suffered together. When one of us saw that the other looked exhausted or close to the breaking point, we would do whatever was necessary to recharge them. When I reached this point, Sara would often hold on to my hand as tight as she could and look directly into my eyes, calming me down. She'd also massage my shoulders, seemingly lifting the weight of the world from them. I likewise did the same for her.

With her gone, though, there was noone there to bring my mind back to the task at hand. I just sat there hour after hour learning nothing, my mind fried. My only thoughts were of Sara and how she had betrayed me. That semester for the first time, I went into the exams not caring if I passed or failed. Somehow I was able to survive, just barely passing. Nevertheless, this accomplishment provided little comfort.

The end of exams just brought new mountains to climb. At the time, I felt as if I was going to try to climb Mount Everest in flip flops and briefs. The next obstacle was graduation. Where previously I had looked upon it as a time of celebration, now it was just a painful reminder of what I had lost. Sara and I were supposed to celebrate it together. We had talked about taking a world cruise. Sadly, those plans were all now moot. I just sat there in my cap and gown, sobbing as I was treated to the glorious sight of happy couple after happy couple, prancing up together to receive their diplomas. As an added bonus, many of the graduates carried their children with them onto the stage. As I watched this, I just wanted to die. Life no longer meant anything to me.

Afterwards, I saw Sara smiling gleefully with Beau as she took her coveted photos, surrounded by a myriad of supposed friends. I watched as she embraced her ethics professor, thanking him for the prestigious position he had just procured for her. Thoroughly disgusted, I walked right past her without uttering a word.

That night as I lay in my bed hoping for a sleep that would never come, I was greeted by a sudden barrage of heaven's tears. I stumbled to my feet, just to find the windows bleeding a deluge of mockery. I quickly grabbed a mop and bucket, yet they proved totally ineffective. For every ounce I removed, ten more cascaded down the walls. I felt like I was trying to bail the ocean from a sinking ship, using just a tea cup.

As the water rose to my knees, I noticed my umbrella and diploma bobbing in the surf, both utterly useless. The purpose of an umbrella is to keep you dry during a rainstorm, yet they do little good if the storm brews from within. Likewise, I had obtained my degree to give Sara the things she so deserved, never pondering the fact that she might not be there to enjoy them. Regrettably, in the time it had taken to procure the items, their purpose had become moot.

The rest of that night was spent just standing there inanely, as it rained in my apartment. Each drop proved a painful reminder of what I had lost. I used to love the rain. As a child I would run through the streets as the rains poured down upon me, renewing my spirits from the hell I called home. Perhaps its greatest quality was its ability to clear out the masses. I could roam through the parks or walk on the pier, unencumbered by my sightseeing, smoke-breathing brethren. During my childhood, I used to think that the masses would sink into the sidewalks at the first drop of rain, just to pop out when the sun began to shine. Sadly, with age I realized how right I had been.

Since the betrayal, I rued the rain. It was a constant reminder of the night we first met. I remembered how beautiful she looked that first night, the rain dripping down her hair as we talked the night away. Along with my heart, she had stolen my love of the rain. The next morning I just wandered the streets, trying to get over the fact that it had actually rained in my apartment! After losing Sara, I thought I'd never again be surprised by life, just to be proven wrong by a rogue indoor rainstorm.

The days after graduation were spent sitting in a dank room, supposedly studying for the Bar exam. The Bar exam is the exam you must pass in order to be able to practice law in a given state. At that point, I could care less about practicing law. Nevertheless, I had paid for this review course months ago, when things like this seemed important.

So there I sat, hour after hour, wasting away in a law school room. I tried to concentrate as I watched the video tape. It was a tape of some professor droning on endlessly about some tedious subject area. A month passed in which every day seemed the same. I would go into this room and sit there, supposedly listening to what they were saying but retaining nothing. My only thoughts were of Sara. Instead of studying and practicing for this exam, I just sat there during the day and drank at night. Every night I would pass out wishing for a quick and painless death, just to wake up to the horror of a new day. Amazingly, the first week of July would spell an end to this monotonous pattern.

As part of the review course, we were given a simulated exam. This was supposed to reveal our weaknesses, in the hope that we would correct them. I miserably failed this exam, yet it brought little change to my demeanor. That night I sat in my apartment drinking Merlot, the rains pouring down as God entertained Himself with another riveting round of "let's torment Roger."

My bottle proved little distraction as my eyes were glued to the window, waiting for my soul to once again be raped by this foul beast. Utterly disgusted by this never ending pattern, I rammed myself through the window, falling three stories to the garden below. Inevitably, I survived, suffering only a few scrapes and bruises. As the rains poured down upon me, my body covered in mud and animal excrement, I realized this was not the ending I wanted. Yes, I had erred by trusting her, yet I had already paid with my heart. I did not have to let this one mistake in judgement consume my career as well as my life.

I picked myself up from the mud and shit, washed myself off, and started anew. I now had a purpose in life, it was to pass the Bar exam. My mind suddenly became clear, as I worked virtually twenty-four hours a day striving to reach my goal. My mornings were spent listening to the video taped lectures. For the first time, my mind began to actually retain the information. My afternoons were spent out on the pier with the wind blowing through my hair as I went over sample essay after sample essay. My nights were spent hunched over my computer screen, answering sample fact pattern after sample fact pattern. My mind became hungry for knowledge, retaining everything I came across. For the first time in what seemed an eternity, I was doing something purely for myself. Consequently, I dedicated every remaining moment to accomplishing that task.

The Bar exam brought with it the first moment of cheer since Sara's betrayal. After the first day, I walked home trying to hold back the smile from my face. Day one had been a success. Every essay consisted of a subject area that I was well prepared for. Day two was similar to the first. Once again there had been no surprises.

Passing the Bar had lifted a great weight from my shoulders. I felt as if the world had tried to step on me, yet I had thrown them off. I had a new zest for life. I was ready to find a job and put Sara behind me. I felt virtually invincible. I had taken life's best hits and was still standing. I vowed that I would never again let anything hurt me. This turned out to be one of the few vows I could not keep, as my invincibility would be short lived.

THE CARROT AND THE MULE

Almost three weeks after passing the Bar, I received a call from Sara. It was the first time I had heard her voice since Olympus and the sound of it made me cringe. She was calling from the hospital and wanted me to pay her a visit. I asked her what had happened but she refused to tell me, unless I visited her. At that moment every vibe in my body told me not to go. Of course I went.

I arrived at the hospital to find Sara laying in her bed. Across her face was a huge scar. She told me that a couple of weeks ago, she and Beau were taking the subway to a party in the city. As she exited the train, she suddenly felt a sharp sting across her face. A gang member, as some sort of initiation rite, had slashed her with a rusty razor. It seems the girl was jealous of her looks and thus selected Sara as her victim. The cut had required sixty-six stitches, permanently scarring her face.

Upon learning that no amount of surgery would make much of a difference, her beloved Beau dumped her immediately. Also while first acting compassionate, her new so-called friends, finding the sight of her to be unpleasant, soon abandoned her. Left alone, Sara stopped eating and soon collapsed from malnutrition. This is why she was in the hospital.

"Roger," she cried, "don't look at me. I'm too hideous to see."

"Whatever," I replied sarcastically.

"You're still hurt, aren't you? Roger, I'm sorry," she whispered. "I made a colossal mistake. I was taken in by Beau and his friends. Can you ever forgive me?"

"Of course I forgive you, Sara," I replied softly.

"Really," she cried.

"Really," I whispered.

"Then we're back together again," she chirped happily.
"No, we're not," I replied coldly.
"But you just said you forgave me."
"I do," I stated.
"I don't understand," she said, looking quite puzzled.
"I do forgive you, Sara," I told her. "However, that does not mean that we could ever be together again. When I look into your eyes, I no longer see the woman I loved and trusted. I just see the back of Beau's head. No, Sara; we could never be together again, because I will never be able to trust you again," I stated matter-of-factly.
"Liar!" she howled. "You're just like all the rest. It was all about looks and now that they're gone, so are you. Get out of here."
"No, Sara," I shouted vehemently. "It was never about looks. I loved you for you. You're the one who chose the superficial life. I offered you a life where I would love you forever, not because of your looks, but because of your heart and soul. It was you who chose style over substance. You're the sellout. You gave up everything that made you special for instant gratification. I warned you when you did it, that it would last at maximum seven years and could end sooner. You chose to take that risk. Now you have to live with the consequences. As the saying goes, "You made your bed, now you have to die in it," I replied slyly.
"But, it wasn't my fault; they tricked me into it," she pleaded.
"No, they didn't," I replied coldly. "You knew exactly what you were doing. Don't try to give me that excuse. I know you too well. We are all responsible for our own actions. Even though they may have tempted you, it was still your choice. As you once said, you're a big girl and can make your own decisions, or don't you remember telling me that?"
"I do, but I was wrong," she whimpered.
"I'm sorry," I said. "It's too late."
"Then why did you come here, Roger? Did you just want to rub my nose in it?" she hollered.
"No, I came here because I had to."
"What does that mean, you had to?" she asked with disdain.

"It means what it says, I had to. Have you ever heard the story of the carrot and the mule?" I queried.

"No," she replied.

"Then listen," I told her. "There once was a farmer who owned a mule, he had bought to pull a plow. Now when a farmer wants a mule to pull something and it refuses, they usually try to trick it into moving. They do this by hanging a carrot or an apple on a string in front of the mule, just beyond the reach of its mouth. When the mule tries to bite it and can't, it moves forward pulling the plow.

"Now when the farmer brought his mule home and attached it to the plow, it refused to move. The farmer tried everything. He hung many carrots and apples, but nothing worked. He then took a whip and hit the mule, yet still nothing. The farmer, he was at a loss. He did not know what to do. He bought a virtual cornucopia of fruits and vegetables, all to no avail.

"Then one day just as he was getting ready to send the mule to the glue factory, he noticed it seemed to be staring at one particular carrot. This carrot had just been picked and was sitting on top of a basket. The farmer, seeing this, took the carrot and tied it in front of the mule. Miraculously, the mule started to pull the plow. The mule pulled and he pulled as hard as he could, alas he could not catch the carrot.

"That night back in the barn, the farmer filled the mule's trough with shiny new carrots, but the tired and hungry mule refused to eat.

"Seeing this, the horse said, 'Mr. Mule, you look hungry and tired, why don't you eat your carrots?'

"'I don't want these carrots, I want my carrot,' the mule responded.

"'Why?' the horse asked.

"'Because, my carrot is special,' the mule replied.

"'I did not see any difference,' the horse countered skeptically.

"'But, I do and that's really the only opinion that matters to me,' the mule stated frankly.

"The next day, the mule once again pulled as hard as he could, but again he failed to reach the carrot. That night, the mule could hardly move. It was both exhausted and starving, but once again it would not touch the shiny new carrots in its trough.

"'Mr. Mule, that carrot you are chasing is starting to dry up, while these new carrots are full of juice. Why don't you eat them?' the horse barked, quite annoyed.

"'I told you, I want my carrot,' the mule replied.

"'Mr. Mule,' the horse shot back. 'I don't know why you would want that stale shriveled up old carrot, instead of these new fresh ones. Nevertheless, I do know from the looks of you that if you don't eat tonight, tomorrow you will die,' the horse stated matter-of-factly.

"'I know,' said the mule. 'However, that fact changes nothing. I would rather die than let anything else touch my mouth.'

"'But why?' the horse snapped dumbfounded. 'I see nothing special in that carrot.'

"'You don't have to,' the mule replied. 'I do.'

"The next day, the mule, hardly able to move, made one last futile lunge towards the carrot, collapsed into the dirt and died."

"What is that supposed to mean?" Sara shouted sarcastically.

"It means what it says," I replied calmly.

"I have no idea what that means. Just tell me why you came," she yelled angrily.

"I came for the same reason that the mule chased after the carrot, even though he knew his pursuit of it would ultimately lead to his downfall."

"Why is that?" she stated coldly.

"Because, in you I see something noone else does. That's why I came, even though I knew seeing you would hurt me. However, this is where it ends," I replied adamantly.

"What ends?" she asked.

"We end," I replied. "I refuse to end up like the mule. I will not let my love for you destroy me, Sara. Goodbye forever," I replied sadly, as I began to walk out.

"Roger," she screamed. "If what you said is true, you can't leave me. Just like the mule, you will come back. You will have to."

"No, Sara," I barked. "It is because I love you that I will not come back. The Sara I love is that kind intelligent creature who's heart is true. If I came back, how could I be sure that you wouldn't just leave me for the next Beau who came along? I mean it would be a no lose situation. If he left you, I'd always be there to fall back on. If there was no price for your sin, it would forever linger on your soul. No, Sara; it is because I love you that I must leave you. It is the only way to show you the true cost of being a superficial person and perhaps save your soul from condemnation," I preached.

This proved the most difficult decision of my life. I had been given a second chance, all I had to do was betray my conscience and take it. My decision seemed simple, given the fact that I had spent my entire life making the moral choice, just to have it smite me. Sadly, the cost of true love is eternal devotion. Once again, like a lemming over a cliff, I followed my conscience and walked out. This was a path I vowed to never again take. The rest of my life would be dedicated to me. I would become rich and powerful, never again longing for the woman I had just given up.

The next day I interviewed for a junior associate position at a small firm. I went into it beaming with confidence, the entire time telling them why they needed me. Not surprisingly they gave me a job on the spot. While my days were spent working for the firm, my nights were busy moonlighting as a solo practitioner. I did wills, divorces, settlement agreements, and anything else I could get my hands on. By the end of the year, I had paid off my loans and bought my first apartment building. It was not the biggest building in the world but it made a profit.

For the next ten years, I spent every moment of my life making money. By the age of thirty-five, I had accumulated a net worth of over one hundred million dollars. I quit my job at the firm and started my own corporation. I owned over one hundred buildings and several resorts. The reason I was able to make so much money was because all my profits went back into the corporation.

My first leisure purchase was a small sailing boat. It was nothing like my yacht of course, but it had the same benefit. Soon I amassed a fleet of ships with *Inner Peace* as the gem of my collection. All this was done to forget Sara. Unfortunately having met perfection, no other woman would do. While most of them only wanted me for the money, even the ones who seemed to care, in my eyes were not fit to lick the boots of the perfection I called Sara.

As for the survivors of Olympus, Mary was executed seven years later to the dismay of both women's rights and anti-death penalty lobbyists. On the bright side of things, her death saw the birth of the "Battered Woman's Defense" as well as the enforcement of stronger domestic violence statutes. As for Mary's myriad of children, they were separated and placed in foster care, scattered throughout the country. Some were adopted by loving families, while others were abused and tossed aside, to the delight of therapists and television talk show hosts alike.

Mr. Ravenport lived the remaining three years of his life a complete recluse, hiding from the scorn of his beloved friends.

He died apparently from a single self-inflicted gunshot wound to the head, although it was three months before his lawyer noticed him missing. Hortance eventually found him sitting in his bedroom chair facing the ocean, the windows wide open.

Sweet little Susie didn't have much time to enjoy her inheritance. I'd like to say that she became a prosecutor of sex offenders and a champion of woman's rights in Peru, but this would be nothing more than a fairy tale. In reality, Susie failed to learn from the lessons of her youth, foolishly trying to drown them out with drugs and alcohol. She died a crackwhore at the tender age of fourteen; murdered in some rat infested hotel room by a disgruntled John.

Over the years Sara would call me many times, yet I refused to answer any of them. My answering machine became littered with her pleas. Eventually, she got the message and stopped calling. Every now and then, I would spot someone who looked like her, but it wasn't. I don't know what happened to her and I don't want to know. I just hope that she had a happy life and did not waste her time catering to the whims of the masses. I thought that I was finally free of her. I had my yacht and my many estates to occupy my time. In an attempt to validate my life, I filled my bed with princesses and supermodels. They all failed to mend my broken heart.

EPILOGUE

As the waves crashed over the now powerless dinghy, my hands clutched tightly to the photo of Sara. With one great swoop, a wave lifted the dinghy high into the air and then slammed it down into the sea. I was pulled deep into the depths of the cold salty brew and thought that it was finally over. Just as quickly another wave tossed me back up. I found myself floating on top of the waves, both my yacht and the dinghy nowhere in sight.

I looked down and saw the crinkled photo of Sara clinging to my hand. I realized I had failed. Everything I had accomplished—the yacht, the buildings, the money—all for nothing. I had created them in the hope that they would end my thoughts of Sara, yet here I was being tossed about the ocean like a cork and the only thing I held on to was the photo of Sara.

My love for Sara after all these years was still as strong as ever. I had tried to fool myself into believing that I could get over her. I thought that I was stronger than the mule. I had hoped that since my actions were made with her best interests in mind, she would not haunt me. Yet the photo in my hand proved otherwise. All the old pain came roaring back.

"God," I yelled. "You win. I never wanted to fight you, but you win!"

I realized that I could not force God to love me. Nevertheless, I was not done yet. There was still one way that I could put an end to God's torture and it was time to do it. I let the photo slide from my hand and watched as it disappeared into the murk. I slipped out of my life vest, allowing myself to sink with it. Peace would finally be mine. Wretchedly, even this proved too much to ask. Just as the ocean's bitter elixir rushed down my nose and throat, burning my eyes and clogging my lungs, I was tossed high into the air and flung back into the sea. This sequence repeated itself for what seemed to be an eternity. Each time I felt the air rushing from my body, I was tossed back up. Finally, I felt myself being tossed higher than I had ever been before and was slammed down into the rocks. I felt an enormous rush of pain and then nothing.

    I awoke to find myself lying on the shore. The storm was over. The tide gently brushed against my legs, then receded into the sea. I was on dry land. My arm and ribs felt like they had been broken, yet I was still alive. I looked down as I felt something stuck in my shirt. Painfully, I reached down and pulled it out. It was the photo of Sara.